Sirens sounded in the distance.

"Lillie, the police are coming. You don't want them to find you here."

Reason tangled through her fear.

"I'm going to let you go. Leave the room. Take the back road. Meet me at the truck stop one exit north on the highway." His hand eased up ever so slightly. "Do you understand?"

She nodded.

He drew away from her and stood.

Scampering to her feet, Lillie raced for the door and threw it open. Light filtered into the darkness. She turned, seeing the special agent bend down and pick up something from the rug.

Dawson Timmons was a fool to think she would meet him anywhere except at the military police headquarters on post.

"You dropped something, Lillie." The key dangled from his hand.

The sirens screamed in the distance. Not much time to get away.

Books by Debby Giusti

Love Inspired Suspense

DEBBY GIUSTI

is a medical technologist who loves working with test tubes and petri dishes almost as much as she loves to write. Growing up as an army brat, Debby met and married her husband—then a captain in the army—at Fort Knox, Kentucky. Together they traveled the world, raised three wonderful army brats of their own and have now settled in Atlanta, Georgia, where Debby spins tales of suspense that touch the heart and soul. Contact Debby through her website, www.debbygiusti.com, email debby@debbygiusti.com, or write c/o Love Inspired Suspense, 233 Broadway, Suite 1001, New York, NY 10279.

The General's Secretary

Debby Giusti

Love Inspired

Recycling programs
for this product may
not exist in your area.

™ LOVE INSPIRED BOOKS

ISBN-13: 978-0-373-44521-9

THE GENERAL'S SECRETARY

Copyright © 2013 by Deborah W. Giusti

www.LoveInspiredBooks.com

Printed in U.S.A.

Cast your cares on the Lord and He will sustain you;
He will never let the righteous be shaken.
—*Psalm* 55:22

This story is dedicated to
our brave men and women in uniform.
May the Lord protect them from harm.

To my wonderful husband and beautiful family.
Thank you for your love and support.

To the Seekers who make the journey so much fun.

To my critique partner Anna Adams.

To Emily Rodmell, my editor,
and Deidre Knight, my agent.
Thank you!

ONE

Lillie Beaumont gasped for air and fought her way through the dream that came too often. Her heart pounded a warning as she blinked open her eyes, allowing the dark outline of her bedroom to sweep into focus. She lifted her head off the pillow and anticipated the distant thunder before the sound reached her ears.

Low. Rumbling. Menacing, like cannon fire at nearby Fort Rickman, Georgia.

Weeding her fingers through the sheets, she grasped for anything that would calm her spinning stomach and racing pulse.

Another rumble, this time closer.

Then another and another in rapid succession, each encroaching on her space, her air, her life.

The thunder escalated, its cadence steady like the giant footfalls of an evil predator, stalking an unsuspecting prey. Only Lillie wasn't oblivious to its approach. She knew the storm, felt it in her inner being, breathed it into her soul where she battled the terror and torment of a thousand deaths.

Another volley. Her airway constricted. She touched her throat, yearning to be free of the stranglehold of fear that wrapped around her neck.

Don't cower. Face your phobia. The words of reason echoed in her head.

"Something happened before she came to us," her foster parents had told concerned friends after taking Lillie into their home when she was a child. "Our little girl is terrified of storms."

She wanted to laugh at the understatement. Instead, tears trickled from the corners of her eyes.

The musky scent of wet earth and damp air seeped through the partially open window and filled her nostrils, like the cloying odor of that night so long ago. Eyes wide, she stared into the darkness, anticipating the next bright burst of lightning.

A blast of thunder rocked her world, hurling her from the bed. She ran, as she always did, her footfalls echoing on the hardwood floor. No matter how much she longed to ignore the gathering storm, she had no control over the memories that made her relive the terror of that night so long ago.

In her mind's eye, she was once again four years old.

"Mama," young Lillie had cried, longing to be swooped into her mother's outstretched arms.

Instead, *he* had opened the bedroom door.

"Go back to bed, child."

The door had closed, leaving Lillie alone in the hallway, huddled in a ball, shivering with fear, tears streaking her face and trembling body.

Another round of thunder, followed by a kaleidoscope of light that blinded her eyes and made the past fade and the present come back into focus.

Finding the corner, the twenty-nine-year-old Lillie crouched, knees to her chest, heart on a marathon race as thunder continued to bellow. Rain pummeled her copper roof, the incessant pings reminding her of the gossip of the townspeople after her mother's remains had been found fifteen years ago.

Murdered. Sealed in a steel drum. Buried beneath the earth.

"Mama," she whimpered, trying to be strong enough to fight off the memories.

Outside, the storm raged as if good and evil battled for her soul, only she was too weak, too crazed, to fight off the attacks.

A pounding.

Close, persistent. *Rap, rap, rap.*

"Lillie?"

Someone called her name.

"Lillie, open the door."

"Mama?"

She ran to the front of the house, undid the lock and flung open the door. Frigid rain stung her face, soaking her pajamas and mixing with her tears.

"Help me, Lillie."

A man she knew only from newspaper photos stood before her. Mid fifties, with gray, rumpled hair and weather-worn skin stretched across a bruised and bloodied face. Doleful eyes, swollen, suffering, seemingly entreated her to forget the past and think only of his need. "They...they found me...beat me."

His hand stretched to hers. A small metal key dropped into her palm.

"I uncovered information. The...the answers I've been looking for," he said.

She took a step back.

"I never—" He shook his head. "Your mother—"

A shot rang out.

He gasped, his face awash with pain. "Free us..." He reached for her. "Free us from the past."

Slipping through her fingers, he collapsed onto the rain-drenched step. She screamed, seeing not only her own bloodied hands but also the battered body of her mother's killer.

The phone call dragged Dawson Timmons from a dead sleep. Flipping on the bedside lamp, he rubbed his hand over his face and raised the receiver. "Special Agent Timmons."

"Sorry to wake you, sir." Corporal Raynard Otis from the Criminal Investigation Division.

"What's the problem, Ray?"

"Agent Steele is on duty tonight, sir, but he's tied up, handling a possible overdose, and we're short-staffed since Agents Patterson and McQueen were transferred."

With the recent reduction in force, the whole army was short-staffed. "I'm aware of the situation, Ray. Plus, the chief's on leave until Monday."

"Yes, sir. That's why Agent Steele asked that I contact you." The corporal's voice was strained. "The Freemont police just notified us about a shooting."

"Military personnel?"

"Negative, sir. But the location has bearing."

"Fort Rickman?"

"No, sir. Freemont."

"What's the tie-in?"

"The house where the shooting took place belongs to the general's secretary."

Dawson groaned inwardly, dropped his feet to the floor and stood. "General Cameron's secretary? The commanding general?"

"Yes, sir. The deceased pounded on the secretary's door in the middle of the storm. She answered the knock just before the victim was shot."

"A drive-by shooting?"

"I'm not sure, sir."

"We're talking about Lillie Beaumont?"

"Affirmative."

"Was she hurt?"

"Negative, sir."

"The victim…" Dawson swallowed, hoping to keep his voice level and free of inflection. "Do you have a positive ID?"

"Granger Ford. The guy was serving time for the murder of Ms. Beaumont's mother. Fifteen years ago he was tried and found guilty. His case was recently reviewed, and new DNA testing exonerated him. Ten days have passed since he got out of prison in Atlanta. Now he's dead."

Dawson hung his head. Ringing filled his ears. His stomach soured, and for an instant, his world went dark. Granger had called him three nights ago. Not that Dawson had expected or wanted the phone call from his past.

"Shall I notify the staff duty officer at post headquarters?" Ray asked.

"Let headquarters know, and call General Cameron's aide as well. Tell him I'll check out the situation and report back to the general when I return to post."

Dawson would tell the commanding general what the Freemont police had determined about the shooting and Lillie Beaumont's involvement in the case. He wouldn't reveal the truth about Granger Ford and the child he had fathered thirty-one years ago. A little boy raised by an unwed mother who had hardened her son's heart to his drifter dad.

Dawson could forgive his mother's bitterness, but he never forgave his father's rejection. Now, with his death, the truth would come out. The last thing Dawson wanted was for the military to know his father was a murderer.

The storm had subsided by the time Dawson climbed behind the wheel of his Camry. Twigs and leaves cluttered the roadway as he left post and headed to the far side of Freemont, where Lillie lived. Turning his headlights to high beam, he pressed down on the accelerator and reached for his cell phone.

"I'm on my way into town," Dawson said when Jamison Steele answered. Working together, the two agents had formed a strong friendship. Trust ran deep, and just days earlier Dawson had told Jamison about his past and the father he had never met.

"Otis said you agreed to handle the shooting." Jamison let out a breath. "Look, I'm sorry about what happened and that you have to be the one to handle the case."

"It's not like Granger and I had a relationship. The last thing he wanted was a kid. My mother said he hightailed it out of town as soon as she told him she was pregnant. I never met him."

"Still, it puts you in a difficult spot. I'll explain the situation to Chief Wilson when he gets back to work on Monday."

Dawson pursed his lips. "No need. I can fight my own battles. Besides, tonight should be fairly straightforward. I'll ensure the Freemont cops handle the case appropriately. Once I share the information with General Cameron concerning his secretary, I'll file my report and move on to the next case."

"It's Friday, Dawson. I'm hoping the weekend is crime-free."

"Which might be wishful thinking."

Jamison hesitated. "Have...have you told anyone else about your dad?"

"I didn't see the need." Dawson stared into the roadway ahead. "Of course, his death changes everything."

"We'll talk at the office."

"Roger that."

Dawson disconnected and shook his head with frustration. Granger had made a huge mistake visiting the daughter of the woman he was supposed to have murdered. From what Dawson had pieced together about his wayward father, Granger's life had been as littered as the pavement with a series of wrong places, wrong times. Exactly what tonight felt like—a wrong turn that could end up detouring Dawson off the straight course he had chosen for his career in the army.

When he saw the secretary's house in the distance, his gut tightened. Police lights flashed from the driveway. The crime-scene crew hovered around the front porch, where a man's body lay spotlighted in the rain. Maybe this homicide wouldn't be as cut-and-dried as he had first imagined.

Pulling to a stop, Dawson sucked in a deep breath before he stepped into the wet night. His left leg ached. More than a year had passed since he'd taken a bullet, but the pain remained and grew more insistent with the cold weather.

He rubbed his hands together and grabbed the keys from the ignition, his mouth dry. Steeling himself against any unwanted rush of emotion, he approached the crime-scene tape and held up his identification to the closest cop.

"CID, from Fort Rickman. Who's in charge?"

The guy pointed to the house. "Head through the kitchen. Sergeant Ron Pritchard's inside with Ms. Beaumont."

"Is she a suspect?"

The cop shrugged. "All I know is that we found her huddled in the hallway, crying like a baby."

Dawson hesitated for a moment and then glanced down at the victim's twisted body. Regret washed over him. This wasn't the way life should end. Granger had been shot in the back, probably with a forty-five caliber hollow point from the appearance of the wound.

In stark contrast to the grisly death scene, beds of yellow pansies edged the small front stoop. Ignoring the flowers, Dawson circled the house, picking his way through the wet grass. The back porch, trimmed in white latticework, was graced with more winter blooms that danced in the wind, oblivious to the crime that had recently been committed.

Stepping into the kitchen, he opened his navy windbreaker and wiped his shoes on the small entry rug. The smell of the wet outdoors followed him inside and mixed with the homey scent of pumpkin and spice. A large melon-colored candle sat on the counter near a bouquet of yellow mums and a plaque that read, *God bless this home and all those who enter.*

The irony wasn't lost on Dawson, yet surely death hadn't been Granger's just reward. The estranged son might have argued the point before the phone call, before Granger had asked forgiveness. Something Dawson hadn't been able to give. Now he wasn't sure how he felt. A little numb, a bit confused, even angry. Long ago, he had realized it was better not to feel anything than to feel too much.

Entering the living area, he signaled to the officer in charge, held up his badge and nodded as the local cop continued to question the woman huddled on the couch.

Lillie's life had been inexplicably intertwined with Dawson's, although he doubted she was aware her mother's killer had a son. They'd never been introduced, but Dawson had seen her on post. It was hard not to notice the tall and slender secretary. Usually she was stylishly dressed and perfectly coiffed. Tonight wild, honey-brown tresses fell across the collar of what appeared to be flannel pajamas. Even from where he stood, Dawson noticed the blood spatters on the thick fabric.

She turned, hearing him behind her.

He hadn't expected her eyes to be so green or so lucid. She wore her pain in the knit of her brow, in the downward tug on her full lips, in the tear-streaked eyes whose sadness wrapped around his heart. His breath hitched, and time stood still for one long moment.

Pritchard asked another question. She turned back to the lead cop, leaving Dawson dangling. He straightened his neck, trying to work his way back to reality.

Long ago, Dawson had learned to weigh everything, never to take a chance. He put his faith in what he could do and affect and impact, not on emotions that left him hanging in thin air.

"The middle of a stormy night." Pritchard restated the last question. "Yet you opened your door when Mr. Ford knocked?"

"I…ah…" She searched for an answer.

"Do you always open your door to strangers, Ms. Beaumont?" Pritchard pressed.

She shook her head. "Of course not, but— "

Once again, she glanced at Dawson, as if asking him to clear the confusion written on her oval face.

"Had you been asleep?" Dawson knew better than to prompt a witness, yet the question sprang from his lips before he could weigh the consequences.

She nodded, her brow raised and lips upturned for the briefest of moments. "I was dreaming. The knock sounded. Before I realized what I was doing, I was staring at him through the open doorway."

Pritchard cleared his throat and jotted her answer in a notebook. After recording the statement, he glared at Dawson. "I'm finished questioning Ms. Beaumont. If there's anything you want to ask her, go right ahead. I'll be outside."

Dawson read between the lines. Pritchard didn't want his interrogation compromised by a newcomer from post. A subtle reprimand, perhaps? Not that Dawson would be intimidated by a small-town cop.

As Pritchard left through the kitchen, Dawson took a seat on the chair next to Lillie and held up his identification.

"Special Agent Dawson Timmons, ma'am. I'm with the Criminal Investigation Division at Fort Rickman. The Freemont Police Department is handling the murder investigation, but the CID was called in because you work on post. I'm here as a liaison between the local police and the military."

"Does…does General Cameron know what happened?" Lillie asked.

"He's being notified."

"I don't want anything to—"

"To jeopardize your job? I don't see how that could happen. Unless your position as the general's secretary has a bearing on this crime."

"No, no." She held up her hand. "This has nothing to do with General Cameron."

"What does it involve, Ms. Beaumont?" He leaned closer. "May I call you Lillie?"

She nodded. "You're not from around here?"

"Georgia born and raised, but my home's in Cotton Grove, close to the Florida border."

She swallowed, the tendons in her graceful neck tight. "I don't know where to start."

"How 'bout at the beginning."

She tucked a strand of hair behind her ear. "I was born in Atlanta and moved to Freemont with my mother when I was a baby. We lived in a remote area, not far from the highway."

Dawson pulled a notebook and pen from his pocket.

"My…my mother disappeared when I was four." Lillie's voice was weak. She cleared her throat. "Most folks thought she had abandoned me and returned to Atlanta with a man." She shrugged. "Her lover. Sugar daddy. Whatever you want to call him."

"Granger Ford?"

"No. The man she was seeing at the time."

"How can you be sure it wasn't Granger?"

"There was a storm the night she disappeared. The thunder awakened me. I was frightened and ran to my mother's bedroom."

Dawson's could envision young Lillie, green eyes wide with fear, golden-brown hair tumbling around her sweet face, scurrying down a darkened hallway.

"The door opened and he…he told me to go back to bed."

"Who was he, Lillie? Do you know his name?"

She shook her head. "But the memory of that night still haunts me, especially when it storms."

"Can you still see his face?"

"Enough to know it wasn't the man who died on my doorstep tonight."

Dawson did the math. "It's been twenty-five years. Appearances change."

She straightened her shoulders. "I know what I saw. The man that night was someone else."

Dawson made a notation on his tablet. "Who raised you after your mother disappeared?"

"Sarah and Walter McKinney took me in. They were an older couple and didn't have children of their own."

"Good people?"

She nodded. The gloom lifted for an instant, revealing her love for her foster parents.

"They wanted to adopt me, but I…" Once again, her eyes sought his. "Maybe it was foolish, but I kept thinking my mother would come back for me."

A nail to Dawson's heart. Did all kids give wayward parents the benefit of the doubt? Must go with the territory. Children wanted to be loved. Hope provided comfort during the dark times. When hope gave out, the reality of life had to be accepted, although some people never made the transition and spent a lifetime looking for the love they never received as a child.

"But your mother didn't come back," Dawson prompted.

Lillie licked her lips as if gathering courage to continue. "When I was fourteen, the river flooded. Not long afterwards, a steel drum was found close to the water, on Fort Rickman property."

Dawson knew about the raging waters that had washed the drum downriver. Dental records confirmed the decomposed body found within was Irene Beaumont, who had gone missing ten years earlier.

"The last time you saw your mother was that stormy night?" He repeated what he already knew to gauge her response.

"That's correct. The night she disappeared."

"You were four years old?"

She nodded.

"Ten years later, your mother's remains were uncovered in a steel drum."

"And found along the river, although I've never visited the actual site. Someday..." Her voice was wistful. "Someday I hope to be strong enough to do just that."

Dawson made another notation on his tablet. "At the time of her disappearance, the townspeople thought your mother had run off to Atlanta with her boyfriend."

"That's...that's what I thought too."

"Finding her remains must have changed local opinions."

"The folks in town started to realize my mother had probably been killed the night she disappeared."

"What did you think, Lillie?"

"I didn't know what to believe."

Dawson heard the confusion in her voice. "What happened next?"

She hesitated before she spoke. "Granger Ford worked for Nelson Construction at the time. The police were investigating the employees and found a picture of my mother under his mattress in the motel where he was staying. They accused him of murder. He was found guilty and sent to jail."

Dawson tapped his pencil against his notepad. "Did you testify at the trial?"

"Supposedly, the case was open and shut. They didn't need to place me on the stand."

Hearing Lillie's response ignited a fire deep within Dawson's belly. From what he had read about the trial, the prosecution had deemed the case open and shut because Granger was a drifter who worked construction when he needed money. Personnel records at Nelson Construction verified the laborer had been on the payroll at the time of Irene Beaumont's disappearance and again when the steel drum, bearing the Nelson Construction name and logo, had been found.

"Do you know anything about the case?" Pritchard stood in the doorway to the kitchen. Dawson hadn't heard him come back inside.

"I did an internet search before I got here." Dawson pocketed his notebook. "Easy enough to access news stories about Granger's release from prison. The article included information about Irene Beaumont's murder."

"The article probably didn't mention that they found the T-shirt she must have been wearing in the drum along with her decomposed body." Pritchard sniffed, unaware of the pained expression on Lillie's face. "Two blood types were identified on the fabric. A-positive, which was Irene Beaumont's blood type, and B-negative. That matched Granger Ford's type."

Anger welled up within Dawson. He had read the transcript of the trial and knew Granger had denied, under oath, ever seeing the bloodied T-shirt or having known the victim.

Dawson made sure his voice was even, his gaze level, before he spoke again. "Yet Mr. Ford was recently released from prison?"

The cocky cop nodded. "Law students from the University of Georgia got wind of the case. They probably hoped to make a name for themselves."

"And the outcome?" Dawson knew too well what the determination had been.

Pritchard pursed his lips. "Something about the blood type being incorrect."

Granger's blood had proved to be a rare "Du"-positive, which would appear negative on an initial rapid-slide test. More definitive blood typing had not been run prior to his trial, and the jury found Granger guilty because of a bloodied T-shirt and an inaccurate blood type. In addition, DNA testing had not been done, and as Lillie had mentioned, a photo of the deceased had been found under the mattress in Granger's motel room, which anyone on the housekeeping or janitorial staffs could have accessed.

"An open-and-shut case, eh?" Dawson couldn't resist the barb that went over Pritchard's head.

"Recent DNA testing verified the B-negative blood on the T-shirt wasn't Granger's. He was released from prison ten days ago, but we're not sure when he arrived in Freemont."

At least seventy-two hours earlier, judging from the phone call Dawson had received when Granger got to town. He kept the information to himself. Pritchard could do his own investigation.

A second cop opened the back door. "Sarge, we're ready to transport the body." Pritchard followed him outside.

Once they were alone, Dawson turned back to Lillie. "What did Granger say when you opened the door tonight?"

"That someone had found him and beat him. I heard the

shot. He fell forward." She stared at her hands. "I...I tried to catch him."

"Did he mention who had found him or did he say anything about your mother?"

She shook her head, but something about her expression told Dawson the secretary knew more than she had revealed.

"Do you think Granger killed your mother?"

She chewed her lip. "I...I don't know."

"Don't know or won't say?"

She hesitated.

"Did Granger contact you after he was released from prison?"

"He called me and wanted to meet. I refused. He said he had information about my mother's death."

"Yet you turned him down?"

"Part of me didn't believe him. The other part wanted to keep the past locked away."

She lowered her gaze and picked at her sleeve.

"There's something else, isn't there?" Dawson asked.

"I know it sounds crazy after a man has died, but..." She pulled in a nervous breath. "I'm worried about what this will do to military and civilian relations in the local area."

"Meaning?"

"You've heard about the new Fort Rickman Museum scheduled to be built on post?"

Dawson narrowed his gaze, trying to make the connection. With construction ready to commence, the huge, multistoried structure promised to be state of the art, with an extensive collection of historical memorabilia and artifacts. In addition, a grand ballroom, auditorium and banquet facilities would attract large-scale events and needed revenue to this part of Georgia.

"I know the museum will be a boon to the local economy," Dawson said, "but I don't see how one man's death could adversely affect the project."

"Funding is the problem." She sighed. "Which sounds so inconsequential compared to the taking of a human life."

"But—"

"That's why I didn't want to meet Granger when he called a few days ago. I knew if anything about my mother's death was brought to light, the construction project could be affected."

Dawson rubbed his hand over his jaw and let out a frustrated breath. "I still don't get the tie-in."

"You're not from around here so you probably don't know Karl Nelson."

"Only by name. Didn't the stolen barrel your mother's body was found in belong to his company?"

"That's right. Nelson Construction Company was the low bid on the museum. Mr. Nelson has been more than generous keeping the projected costs at a minimum."

"He also owns a number of businesses in town?"

"And is known for his charitable contributions. Over the years, he and his father before him have done a lot for the local area. Mr. Nelson has also donated heavily to the museum building fund and has been working with General Cameron to attract more donors. They're hosting a special ceremony on Wednesday to secure the remaining pledges."

Dawson was aware of the event. "The CID, along with the military police on post, will be providing security for the high-profile guests."

Lillie nodded. "General Cameron wants everything to go without a glitch. Mr. Nelson personally assured the donors that Freemont and Fort Rickman are exemplary communities that will showcase the best in Georgia living and draw new businesses and attractions to this part of the state."

"You're afraid the murder investigation could cause the donors to change their minds?"

She nodded slowly, as if struggling to find the words to express her feelings. When she finally spoke, she splayed her hands. "I work in General Cameron's office and am the contact person for those attending the ceremony. A pending murder investigation that involves the company, especially since Granger was killed on my property, could shed the wrong kind of light on Freemont and the project, maybe even on General Cameron. Especially if information leaks out about my mother's murder."

After everything that had happened, Lillie wasn't thinking rationally, but Dawson understood her concern. The museum project had been the talk of the post for months and everyone was eager for construction to commence. Small-town gossip could get out of hand, and with an abundance of charities needing funding, negative publicity could sway donors into changing their minds about supporting the building project.

Before Dawson could offer her reassurance, Pritchard stepped back inside.

"We're ready to wrap things up." He glanced at Lillie. "The front step is sealed off. Some of my men will return in the morning to go over the crime scene again. Use the kitchen entrance until I give you the all clear, and stay in the area in case we have more questions."

"I'm not planning to leave town."

Dawson stood and pulled two business cards from his pocket. He gave one to Pritchard. "The CID office phone number and my personal cell are under my name."

Retrieving the pen from his pocket, Dawson jotted down an additional number on the back of the card he handed Lillie. "I live in the bachelor officers' quarters on post. The handwritten digits are for the direct line to my apartment at the BOQ."

A uniformed cop approached Pritchard. "We found some numbers scratched on a scrap of paper tucked in the victim's jacket."

Pressure pushed on Dawson's chest as Pritchard read from the paper. "Nine-seven-one-four."

Lillie stared at Dawson's business card and silently mouthed the last four digits of his BOQ phone number. Nine-seven-one-four. The same numbers found in Granger's jacket.

She glanced up at Dawson. Her forehead furrowed.

Oblivious to her questioning gaze, Pritchard pulled out his cell. "Might be a portion of a phone number. I'll add the local prefix and see what we get."

Pritchard tapped in the digits and then shook his head as he disconnected. "The number's not in service."

Dawson needed to leave the little house in the woods before the Freemont cop tried the unique prefix for Fort Rickman phone lines.

He turned to Lillie, who continued to stare at him. "Don't hesitate to call me, ma'am, if you think of anything else that might have bearing on this case."

One of her finely arched brows rose ever so slightly. "Shall I use your cell phone or your BOQ number?"

The muscle in Dawson's neck twitched. "My cell."

Lillie knew he was withholding information from Pritchard. Just as she was.

Maybe they could trade secrets.

TWO

The CID agent climbed into his car as Pritchard and his men prepared to leave the area. Instead of returning to Fort Rickman, Dawson turned right out of the driveway and sped along the rain-washed road that headed north toward the interstate. Rounding a bend, he passed under a train trestle and spied the lights from the Hi-Way Motel in the distance.

The triangle of red, green and blue neon pointed toward the one-story brick building that offered small rooms at a modest rate for those who couldn't afford the larger chain motels closer to Freemont. *Vacancy,* the sign flashed, begging for business.

Pulling into the drive, Dawson cut his lights and circled to the rear of the complex. He parked under an oak tree away from the handful of cars in the back lot.

Grabbing a pair of latex gloves from his console, Dawson hustled toward the last room on the far end of the building, the room where his father had said he was staying when he called three days ago. Dawson slipped his hands into the gloves and tried the knob, relieved when it turned.

His eyes adjusted to the darkness. The bed was rumpled, pillows and comforter strewn over the nearby throw rug. Two dresser drawers hung open. An unzipped duffel bag sat on the floor next to a small desk and overturned lamp.

Either a scuffle had ensued or someone had ransacked the room. Maybe both.

Using his cell phone for light, Dawson checked the duffel, finding only underwear and socks. He opened the remaining dresser drawers. Empty except for a hardcover Bible. Standard toilet articles in the bathroom. Two shirts and a pair of jeans hung in the closet.

A car pulled to a stop outside. Footsteps approached on the walkway that edged the rooms. Dawson's pulse kicked up a notch, realizing, too late, he had failed to flip the latch.

Rap, rap, rap.

He glanced at the bathroom that offered no place to hide. The closet hung open. Small, dark, confining. Exactly where he didn't want to go.

A key scratched against the lock. The knob turned.

Sweat pooled around his neck. He didn't have a choice and slipped into the closet's confining darkness. His heart skittered in his chest. He left the door ajar and peered through the crack.

Someone stepped into the room.

Five-seven and slender with shoulder-length hair and big eyes that took in the room with one glance.

Lillie?

The last place Lillie wanted to be was Granger Ford's motel room, but she had thought the key would unlock the door and lead to information about her mother's death.

Three nights ago, Granger had phoned and asked her to meet him here. In hindsight and despite her concern about the museum project, she should have accepted his invitation.

He'd claimed to have answers, which she took to mean information about what had happened on that stormy night so long ago. Obviously, from the disarray, someone had searched the motel room, looking for the information that must have played into Granger's death.

Lillie pulled in a deep breath to calm her runaway pulse. As her eyes adjusted to the darkness, she stepped toward the duffel bag. After rifling through the contents, she opened the dresser drawers. Her fingers rested briefly on the Gideon Bible. *Lord, let me find the truth.*

Granger claimed he had never known her mother and had had nothing to do with her death. Not that Lillie was sure she believed him. Easy enough to beg forgiveness after the fact.

"Go back to bed, child."

Yet Granger's voice wasn't the one she heard in her dreams. Nor was his face the one that returned to haunt her with each passing storm.

Knowing it was only a matter of time before the Freemont police or the muscular CID agent from Fort Rickman found where Granger had been staying, she tugged on the closet door.

A man stood shadowed in the recesses.

Her heart exploded in her chest. She screamed.

Turning to flee, her foot caught on the leg of the bed. She lost her balance.

"Lillie."

Hands reached for her, easing the fall. He took the brunt of the blow as they both crashed to the floor.

She kicked, heard him groan and kicked again.

He pinned her down, the weight of his legs impeding her movement. "I won't hurt you."

She screamed again.

He covered her mouth with his hand. His breath warmed her cheek.

"Lillie, stop." His voice was low, insistent.

She bit his hand.

"Augh," he groaned. "Listen."

Sirens sounded in the distance.

"The police are coming. You don't want them to find you here."

Reason tangled through her fear as she recognized Dawson's voice.

"I'm going to let you go. Leave the room. Take the back road out of the motel. Meet me at the truck stop one exit north on the highway. We need to talk." His hand eased up ever so slightly. "Do you understand?"

She nodded.

He drew away from her and stood.

Scampering to her feet, Lillie raced for the door and threw it open. Light filtered into the darkness. She turned, seeing the special agent bend down and pick up something from the rug.

Dawson Timmons was a fool to think she would meet him anywhere except at military police headquarters on post.

"You dropped something." The key dangled from his hand.

The sirens screamed in the distance. Not much time to get away.

"Meet me at the truck stop," he said again. "We can share information."

The police would never understand how she had known about the motel room and why she had been there with the CID agent. Leaving the parking lot, she headed out the back way.

On the phone, Granger had said he'd been framed. At the time, she hadn't wanted his excuses to buy her sympathy. Now she wasn't sure about anything or anyone, especially the special agent who seemed to be one step ahead of her.

General Cameron had spoken highly of the Criminal Investigation Division on post. A number of big cases had been solved over the past few years because of their hard work. That's why she had felt comfortable sharing her story tonight with the special agent.

Now she wondered if she could trust him. How had he known about the motel room? Could he have been one of the people Granger claimed had framed him? If so, Dawson was the last person Lillie should meet. Yet, he now had the key that might unlock information about her mother's disappearance.

Lillie needed to be smart and careful, which meant having something to hold over Dawson's head if things got ugly. Grabbing her phone, she dialed her private line at work that hooked into the voice mail she checked each morning as soon as she arrived at her desk.

If something happened to her, General Cameron's aide would eventually review the messages. "This is Lillie Beaumont," she said once the call transferred to voice mail.

She glanced at the clock on her dash. "It's four-thirty a.m. I'm on my way to the truck stop at the exit north of town to meet CID Special Agent Dawson Timmons concerning Granger Ford's death. If something should happen to me, question Agent Timmons."

Years earlier her mother had disappeared on a stormy night. She glanced at the leaves and branches strewn across the road. Meeting Dawson could put her own life in danger.

A shiver slipped down her spine. Lillie had to ensure that she wouldn't disappear on this stormy night like her mother.

THREE

Dawson parked on the far side of the truck stop where his car wouldn't be seen from the interstate. Quickly pulling out the wax kit he kept in his glove compartment, he made a mold of Lillie's key. Later, if need be, he could make a duplicate.

Leaving his car, he rounded to the front of the one-story stucco building and glanced at the few cars driving along the highway, their lights cutting through the darkness. The rain had stopped, but a wind blew from the west. He rubbed his bare hands together as he approached the all-night diner and peered through the large windows. Standing behind the counter, a waitress poured coffee for two husky guys in parkas.

Dawson wiped his feet on the doormat, frustrated by the damp cold that gnawed at the old gunshot wound to his leg. He thought of the investigation that had left him injured, hating the ever-present limp and accompanying pain.

Stepping inside, Dawson unsnapped his windbreaker and nodded to the waitress, who raised a pot of coffee. He held up two fingers and pointed to the booth where Lillie sat. She watched him approach the table and slide into the seat across from her.

"Thanks for meeting me," he said, adding a smile to counter her frosty glare.

"You have something that belongs to me," she said in lieu of a greeting.

The waitress approached with two mugs she quickly filled. "You folks want breakfast?"

"Coffee's fine." Lillie dumped a packet of sweetener and a significant amount of cream into her mug.

"Two eggs over easy, hash browns, sausage and biscuits." Dawson eyed Lillie. "You like grits?"

"Of course, but—"

"Make that two orders with grits."

The waitress scurried back to the kitchen.

Lillie raised her brow. "I don't need breakfast."

"Maybe not, but it's been a long night." He glanced at the men at the nearby counter and lowered his voice. "I'm glad you decided to meet me."

She wrapped her fingers around the chunky mug. "Did I have a choice?"

"You could have gone home."

"I need my key."

She held out her hand, palm up, which he ignored.

"You tried the key at the motel," Dawson said, "thinking it would open the door. Evidently Granger didn't tell you what it unlocked when he called you."

She tilted her head and braced her shoulders before she leaned across the table, her voice low. "When did he call nine-seven-one-four, the number on your business card?"

Touché. Ms. Beaumont had a mind and wasn't afraid to use it. He stretched back in the booth. "You've developed a bit of an attitude since you left your house, Lillie. What happened?"

"I realized you may be more of a problem than an asset."

"Which means?"

"I thought I could trust you."

He shrugged. "I'm working for Uncle Sam. I'm trust-worthy."

"Really, Dawson?" She raised a brow and stared at him across the table.

He almost smiled at the cute way her nose turned up and the handful of freckles that dotted her cheeks, neither of which he had noticed earlier. "Let's make a trade. Okay? You go first."

She shook her head. "I've already told you everything."

"Why did Granger pick tonight to stop by your house?"

"He was on the run. As I mentioned, someone found him and beat him."

"But why?"

"Because he was trying to uncover the truth about what happened to my mother." Lillie glanced at the waitress then back at Dawson. "I overheard the prosecuting attorney talking to my foster parents before Granger's trial began. The lawyer was worried the evidence wouldn't be enough to find him guilty. Everyone wanted to pin the crime on someone. Granger was the logical choice."

Dawson's muscles tensed. "Do you know that for sure?"

She leaned in closer. "All I know is someone wanted my mother dead, only I never knew who. At the time, it was easier to believe Granger was guilty."

"And now?"

"Now I want everything to go back to the way it was before Granger knocked on my door." She sighed. "Only there's no going back."

"Why would someone want to kill your mother?"

"I thought it was because of me. That I had done something wrong."

"Which doesn't make sense, Lillie."

"Not to an adult, but children always believe they're at fault when something bad happens."

Dawson thought of his own childhood. For too long, he had blamed himself for his absentee father.

Lillie pointed a slender finger at him. "Now it's your turn, Mr. CID Agent. How are you involved?"

"I'm representing the military in the investigation."

"There's something you're not telling me."

She was right, but Dawson wasn't ready to reveal anything else.

His cell rang. He pulled the mobile phone from his pocket. "Timmons."

"Pritchard here. Thought you might be interested in the latest."

"Hold on a second." Dawson glanced at Lillie. "I need to take this call."

Without waiting for her response, he slid from the booth and hustled outside. The chilly night air swirled around him. He pushed the phone to his ear. "Go ahead."

"The victim rented a room at the Hi-Way Motel. We're there now."

"Did you find anything that has bearing on his death?" Dawson asked.

"A photo cut from the local newspaper of a guy named Billy Everett was hidden in the motel Bible."

The one place Dawson hadn't looked.

"Everett got into trouble a few years back," the cop continued. "The news photo was taken when we hauled him in for questioning. We didn't have enough evidence and eventually had to release him."

"Had he been arrested before?"

"For possession. Did some time. Claimed he had cleaned up his life, but the guy's got problems. Not too smart, and years of abusing drugs haven't helped."

"So why would Granger have his picture?"

"Your guess is as good as mine."

"Do me a favor," Dawson said. "Fax me a copy of the photo."

"Will do."

"Any indication Everett was involved in tonight's shooting?"

"A lamp was overturned, and the bedding was disheveled. Looks like there could have been a scuffle."

Or someone was looking for something, such as a key, which Dawson didn't mention. He raked his hands across his face, needing the coffee he hadn't had a chance to drink.

"If they had argued—" Dawson went along with Pritchard's theory "—why would Granger go to Lillie's house?"

"The guilty always return to the scene of the crime. Irene Beaumont's house burned down years ago, but her daughter was still in town. If Granger killed Irene, he might want her daughter to know about his release from prison."

"Lillie was only four years old when her mother disappeared."

"She heard a man's voice that night," Pritchard said. "Irene Beaumont had a Fulton County license plate on her car when she arrived in Freemont. Initially, folks thought she had gone back to Atlanta with her lover. No mention of a husband. Most people presumed she had never married."

"And left her child home alone?"

"No one said she was the best of mothers."

Small towns were all alike. Similar talk had lived on in Cotton Grove. Hard for a kid who heard what people said behind his mother's back.

Pritchard sniffed. "Of course, all that changed when they found her body."

"Did the motel manager know anything about what happened today?" Dawson asked.

"He saw a guy who matched Everett's description. Red hair and a scar on his right cheek. Hard to miss. Highway Patrol's on the lookout for him. I'll keep you posted."

Dawson disconnected and pocketed his phone as he returned to the booth.

"That was the police, wasn't it?" Lillie wrapped her arms defensively across her chest. "Did they find anything at the motel?"

"A photograph of a guy named Billy Everett was tucked in the Bible. Red hair. Scar on his right cheek. Do you know him?"

She shook her head.

"Pritchard thought there had been a scuffle."

Lillie shrugged. "Granger's face was bloodied, but I got the impression someone had searched the room."

She thought for a moment. Her face clouded. "You were there when I arrived."

Dawson pointed a finger back at his own chest. "You think I messed up the place?"

"You didn't tell Pritchard about the motel room." She held his gaze. "Granger had your BOQ phone number in his pocket. You didn't reveal that either."

"And you failed to mention the key."

"Which belongs to me." Once again, she held out her hand.

Disregarding her request, Dawson stared into her pretty eyes. "Granger knew he had been set up. The case was open and shut, as you mentioned, only because they had a fall guy, a transient construction worker who came to town when he needed money. A guy who didn't have resources to defend himself."

"The court appointed an attorney."

Dawson laughed ruefully. "A lawyer who should have retired years earlier. You probably didn't follow the local news when you were a kid. Not long after the trial, the lawyer was diagnosed with dementia and was placed in a nursing home where he died a bit too soon thereafter."

"If you grew up in Cotton Grove, why were you interested in a murder that took place in Freemont?"

Her question caught Dawson off guard. He looked down at his mug, weighing his response. "I planned on making the army a career. My local library carried the Freemont papers as well as information about Fort Rickman."

Lillie shook her head. "My mother's death had nothing to do with the military. What aren't you telling me?"

He ignored her question. "I still don't understand why Granger would return to Freemont and jeopardize his newfound freedom?"

"He wanted to clear his name, to make good on the past. At least that's what he told me over the phone. He said he'd made mistakes. He'd abandoned someone and wanted to make it up to him."

A muscle in Dawson's neck twitched. "Him?"

"His son."

Inwardly, Dawson groaned. "A son was never mentioned in the news reports. Maybe Granger was lying to get on your good side."

"It's possible." Her bravado faltered. She rubbed her forehead. "Actually, I don't know what to believe. I boxed up all the memories of long ago, hoping I could hide the past. Granger's death forces everything out into the open."

Maybe Lillie understood how he felt growing up as the kid without a dad. Dawson had put the snippets of gossip together. Some people never forgot the drifter who had left his mother pregnant. No name on his birth certificate meant legally Dawson didn't have a father. It didn't mean he didn't know who his father was.

Just as Lillie had indicated, Granger's death forced everything into the open. It was time for the truth.

"You said Granger mentioned having a son." Dawson let out a lungful of pent-up air. "He was talking about me. Granger Ford was my dad."

Her eyes narrowed. "Why didn't you say so earlier?"

"Because I buried the past just like you did."

"I don't believe you." She grabbed her purse and slid from the booth.

He stood and reached for her wrist. "Don't leave, Lillie."

She jerked free of his hold. "You used me to get information."

"I did no such thing." He dug in his pocket and pulled out a twenty-dollar bill. Throwing it on the table, he turned to find the two truckers glaring at him.

The waitress came around the counter. "Is there a problem?"

"The lady's not feeling well."

Dawson hurried after Lillie, but when he stepped outside, all he could see were the taillights of her Honda Civic racing away in the distance.

Climbing behind the wheel of his own car, Dawson pulled out of the lot and backtracked along the winding road. The temperature had warmed somewhat, and a thick fog rose from the wet earth, clouding his view of the roadway.

Lillie said the past had found her. It had found Dawson as well, but the past wasn't the issue. The present was the problem. For a father who never claimed him as his son, Granger's death was liable to change Dawson's life forever—and not for the better.

Lillie drove too fast along the narrow road, wanting to get away from Dawson Timmons. If not for the key, which he still had, she never would have stopped at the diner.

He had hidden the truth from the Freemont police and from her, pretending he had her best interest at heart. All the while, he was gathering information about his father.

She didn't understand anything, including her mixed feelings about the determined CID agent whose eyes were rimmed with sorrow. On one hand, she didn't want to reveal anything to him, then she found herself opening up and saying more than she should.

Coming around the bend, she slowed her speed. Headlights approached, faster than the limit allowed on the twisted back road. She pulled her Honda to the right, hoping to give the speeding vehicle more room.

The glare blinded her for an instant. When her vision cleared, she saw an SUV had crossed the line and was headed straight for her.

Her heart stopped.

She turned the wheel and swerved off the road, narrowly missing a head-on collision.

Her car hit the shoulder and skidded in the wet grass. She lifted her foot from the accelerator and pumped the brakes. Keeping the wheels in line took all her strength.

The engine died, and the Honda rolled to a stop. Heart in her throat, she gasped for air and glanced in her rearview mirror.

A tingle of ice ran down her spine. The SUV that had almost run her off the road had turned around and was racing toward her.

Lord, protect me.

She turned the key in the ignition, relieved when the engine purred back to life, but when she accelerated, the wheels dug into the rain-soft earth. The tires spun over and over again.

"Oh, God, please."

In a flash of motion, the large sport-utility vehicle passed by and then braked to a stop just ahead of where she was stuck in the mud.

A door slammed.

A figure cut through the fog.

Opening her door, she sprang into the wet night and started to run.

Footsteps sounded behind her.

Her heart thumped a warning.

She pushed forward.

Another set of headlights cut through the darkness.

The man behind her swore. He skidded to a halt and ran back to his car.

She flailed her arms, needing to flag down the approaching motorist. The vehicle stopped and someone stepped onto the pavement. A big, burly blond.

Lillie might have made a mistake.

The man who ran her off the road was someone to fear, but the man walking toward her might be as well. How could she trust a man whose father had killed her mother long ago?

FOUR

Dawson saw Lillie spotlighted in the headlights. Fear strained her face. She glanced quickly over her shoulder at the fleeing man and then back at Dawson. She hesitated, as if unsure whether to approach him.

"Lillie." He softened his voice and opened his arms to reassure her. "I'm not a threat. You're safe with me."

Her eyes filled with confusion. Then, as if the fog had lifted, she stepped into his embrace.

Her trembling body molded to him. He drew her closer, touched by her need. As strong as she tried to appear, beneath the facade was a woman who longed to trust someone. Hopefully, to trust him.

Her head nestled into his shoulder. Tears streamed from her eyes as if an emotional dam had given way. Dawson drew her to himself, a desire to keep her safe surging within him. The warmth of her closeness and the silky softness of her hair sent confusing signals to his heart.

He had never experienced anything like this dealing with other investigations. Usually he remained uninvolved and in control, but at the moment, his professional side was playing Russian roulette with his emotions.

His eyes watched the light-colored SUV—maybe an Expedition or Suburban—drive off, wheels screeching in the night as the taillights were enveloped by the fog. The license plate was obscured, but he saw a reflective army decal on the rear bumper. As fast as the maniac was driving, Dawson wouldn't be able to catch up to him, so he kept his arms around Lillie.

"Shhhhh," he soothed, smelling the heady scent of her perfume, a floral mix that made him think of springtime and sunshine—so the opposite of the dark night and heavy fog that surrounded them now. "You're safe. I won't let anyone hurt you."

Except someone wanted to do her harm. Someone who had gunned down Granger because of what he had uncovered. The killer probably thought the ex-con had passed information on to Lillie, information the killer—or killers—didn't want revealed.

Anger bubbled up within Dawson. He wanted to slam his fist into the gut of anyone who tried to hurt Lillie. He had to keep her safe, not just because she worked on post and had a very important boss, but because his own father had put her in danger.

She pulled back and turned her puffy but pretty face toward him. "I…I'm sorry. Usually I'm not this emotional."

"Fear has a way of changing everything, Lillie." He wanted to reassure her. "You were scared. Once the danger passes, the natural response is to release emotion. Tears can be cathartic."

She tried to smile as she wiped her eyes.

He dug his right hand in his back pocket and pulled out a handkerchief, which he held out to her.

"Thanks." She patted the cloth against her cheeks and sniffed again as she attempted to laugh. "I feel silly."

"Don't." He put his hands on her shoulders and turned her toward her car. "Let's see if we can get you back on the road. Tell me exactly what happened."

"The SUV came around the curve too fast. I swerved to avoid a collision."

"The same guy who chased after you?"

She nodded. "When he made a U-turn, I knew he was coming for me. If…if you hadn't stopped…"

She didn't need to finish the sentence. Both of them realized how vulnerable she had been on the back road in the early-morning hours with the heavy veil of fog closing in around her.

"Did you see his face?"

She shook her head. "All I could think about was getting away."

Dawson hadn't recognized the man or his vehicle and would be hard-pressed to provide a description other than a large SUV, either white or beige. He hadn't been able to read the license plate, and the only thing he had seen was the decal.

Keeping his arm around Lillie, he guided her to a safe spot just a short distance from her Honda. Sliding behind the wheel, Dawson started the ignition and eased down on the accelerator, giving the engine enough gas to move the car forward and free of the trough the wheels had dug earlier.

After steering onto the blacktop, he put the gear in Park and opened the door. "Looks like you're good to go. What time do you have to be at your office?"

"Eight o'clock, but I'm usually there by seven-thirty." She glanced at her watch. "I need to change before I head to post."

"I'll follow you."

"I hate to hold you up."

"Not a problem."

"Thank you." She attempted to smile.

"I won't let you out of my sight."

The drive to her house was uneventful, and soon both cars

were parked in her driveway. Ignoring the front entrance, still draped with crime-scene tape, they walked around the house and entered through the kitchen.

Lillie made a pot of coffee, which Dawson sipped as he looked around her living area. The house was nicely furnished with a contemporary couch and love seat and a mix of antique wooden pieces, including an oak sideboard and carved bookshelves.

The inlaid wood and the fine lines of the detailed ornamentation verified the pieces were works of art, which Dawson admired. Ironic that, since Lillie didn't have a family history of her own, she decorated with treasures from someone else's past.

Side tables topped with marble—exquisite rock that added beauty to the room—sat on each side of the couch. A few knickknacks were scattered about, and two framed photographs rested atop the mantel. One showed a beautiful woman with a small child in her arms.

Glancing closer, Dawson recognized Lillie's sweet face and curly honey-brown hair. The other picture was of an older couple. An adolescent Lillie stood with her arms around both of them. Probably the McKinneys, the foster parents with the big hearts and willingness to open their home to a small child who had no one.

Dawson instantly knew he liked both of them. His gaze returned to the other photo. Although the picture had faded, he could see the resemblance between Lillie and the woman holding her, no doubt Irene Beaumont.

Had his father killed her? Dawson's gut tightened. Turning away from the mantel, he headed for the kitchen and refilled his mug.

Outside, the fog had lifted, and as he sipped the coffee, the sun colored the horizon.

"I need to apologize for my actions at the diner."

Dawson turned at the sound of Lillie's voice. She had combed her hair and changed into a stylish dress that hugged her curves and made his breath jam in his throat.

"I…I was only thinking of myself and my job and what's happening at Fort Rickman." Her pretty eyes were filled with compassion. "Your father died this morning. I'm… I'm sorry."

He placed his mug in the sink. "I never knew him. Never talked to him until he called a few nights ago. He… he wanted to meet."

Dawson pulled in a breath. "My father had rejected me all my life, so I rejected him. Only now—" He shrugged, unable to find the words to express the way he felt.

She took a step closer. "Granger wanted to make it up to you. He didn't want his son to be ashamed of him."

Since the trial, Dawson had blocked his father out of his life. He hadn't talked about him or acknowledged him or allowed him into his heart. It was easier to deny him than to accept who his father had been—a convict, a criminal, a killer.

"I went into law enforcement to right the wrongs my father had committed. Now I find out he may not have been the man I thought he was. That's hard to get my mind around."

Dawson glanced out the window, wondering what the new day would bring. If he had made a mistake about his father, maybe there were other things he needed to reconsider, but he couldn't share his feelings with Lillie. Not now. Not when they were involved in a murder investigation. Even if the victim was his dad.

As Lillie watched the confusion play over Dawson's face, the memories from her own childhood bubbled up within her. "After my mother disappeared, I cried myself to sleep night after night. More than anything, I wanted a normal life, someone to love me, to tuck me in when I went to bed and help me get dressed in the morning."

She pulled in a fragile breath. "I was fortunate the Mc-Kinneys took me in. They were patient and loving, but at four years old, I wanted my own mother to wrap me in her arms."

With a rueful smile, she added, "Sometimes I think I never stopped mourning her loss, and as much as I wanted to block out everything that had happened, I feared the Mc-Kinneys would be taken from me as well."

Understanding mellowed Dawson's gaze and made her question why she told him things she had never told anyone else. She reached for her purse, trying to shield herself from what she saw in Dawson's eyes.

"I can't be late for work."

He grabbed her hand. "Lillie."

She stopped and looked up, her breath stalled by his closeness.

"I'm sorry," he said.

She tried to smile. "Life can be a tough place for kids, but I...I shouldn't have mentioned my own problems, Dawson. You have enough of your own."

"You don't have to hide anything from me." His voice was gentle, like the morning mist.

As much as she wanted to believe him, she had spent her whole life covering up the pain of being a child left behind. She couldn't admit the way she really felt to anyone. Especially not to a man whose crystal-blue eyes could see into her heart.

She dug her keys out of her purse and tilted her head, trying to lighten her tone and her expression. "I don't want to keep General Cameron waiting."

Dawson nodded and followed her outside. "You lead. I'll take up the rear."

"Once we get to post, I'll be fine."

He opened her car door. "I'll follow you to your office."

She climbed behind the wheel. He closed the door and gazed through the car window. "Lock your doors," he mouthed.

So like a cop, but she complied with his request, feeling oddly relieved that someone was concerned about her well-being. Dawson was probably just doing his job. No reason for her to jump to any other conclusion, which she continued to tell herself as they entered Fort Rickman and drove toward post headquarters.

Lillie parked close to the building and met up with him on the sidewalk. "Thank you."

His hand touched her back. "I'll follow you inside."

Her cheeks flushed as they hurried along the walkway and climbed the steps. Dawson held the door for her, and her heels clicked along the tile floor.

She stopped in front of the elevator.

"Let's take the stairs," he suggested.

The elevator door opened and she stepped inside. "This will be faster."

He hesitated before joining her. As the door closed, Lillie could tell something was wrong. Dawson's face paled. He licked his lips and clenched his fist until the doors opened on the second floor.

She stepped onto the landing. "I take it you don't like elevators."

"Actually, the problem is confined spaces."

"I'll try to remember that." She pointed him toward the general's suite, located at the far end of the hallway.

Dawson studied the long corridor, probably assessing her safety. Leaving him to do his job, she entered the office and nodded to the general's aide.

"Morning, Mark."

Medium height with broad shoulders and a military haircut, Captain Mark Banks stood near her desk, holding a phone to his ear. Hopefully he hadn't retrieved the message concerning Dawson.

"I was worried, Lillie." He held her gaze longer than necessary.

As much as the aide wanted to be part of her life, Lillie had rejected his advances. She didn't need a relationship with someone with whom she shared an office or worked with on a daily basis.

"The CID called." His brow creased with concern. "They said you were involved in a shooting."

Dawson had evidently completed his hallway security check because, at that moment, he entered the outer office and glanced from Lillie to the general's aide.

Mark squared his shoulders. "You're from the CID?"

"That's right. Special Agent Dawson Timmons." He flashed his identification.

"Lillie's not in trouble, is she?" the aide asked.

"Of course not." She let out a frustrated sigh. Suddenly her life had gotten complicated. "A man was shot. He died. No one knows why he chose my front porch."

As if doubting her overly simplistic explanation, the aide puffed out his chest. "Surely Mr. Timmons has some idea of what happened."

Ignoring the aide's sarcasm, Dawson nodded. "We're working with the Freemont police. At this point, nothing significant has come to light."

Lillie had hoped coming to work today would ease her anxiety. Standing between two men playing a game of one-upmanship made her wish she had called in sick.

The best way to rectify the situation was to send Dawson on his way. "Thank you, Agent Timmons, for all your help. I'll be fine from now on."

He glanced at his watch. "I want to update General Cameron on what happened. I'll stick around until he arrives."

Mark raised his brow. "I thought you didn't have additional information?"

What was it about men? They were always in competition.

Edging away from Mark, she rounded her desk and dropped her purse in the bottom drawer. "The general's tied up this morning, Dawson, but I can pencil you in later."

At that moment, the outer door opened and General Cameron stepped into the office. Mark and Dawson came to attention.

Lillie smiled. "Good morning, sir."

In his early fifties with a square face and receding hairline, the general nodded to the two men and then softened his stern expression as he turned to Lillie. "The staff duty officer called me at home and told me there had been a shooting at your house. You're all right?"

"I was never in danger, besides…" She extended her hand toward Dawson. "Special Agent Timmons arrived shortly after the shooting. He followed me to post to ensure I arrived safely."

The general extended his hand. "Thank you for helping Lillie."

Dawson accepted the handshake. "The Freemont police are handling the investigation, sir. I'll be working with them."

"Any leads?"

"Not at this time."

"Keep me abreast of the situation."

"Will do, sir."

The general nodded to his aide. "Morning, Mark." He then headed through another door that led to his inner office suite.

Lillie pulled out her desk chair. Before she sat down, the

outer door opened again, and Karl Nelson hustled into the office. Forty-something and slightly out of breath, the head of Nelson Construction smacked of small-town wealth in his hand-tailored suit, starched white shirt and red tie.

"I'm early for my appointment with the general, Lillie." Five-ten and wearing twenty extra pounds, Karl approached her desk. "I heard about the shooting. Are you all right?"

"I'm fine, Mr. Nelson, but I wish I could say the same for Granger Ford."

Karl harrumphed. "The man was a murderer. He never should have been released from prison. In my opinion, he received his due."

Dawson flinched. "I beg to differ, sir."

Lillie's stomach tightened. If only Dawson could shrug off the comment and not let the contractor get under his skin.

"What's that?" Karl turned, as if only now realizing the CID agent was in the room.

"Granger Ford was recently released from prison, Mr. Nelson, because of new DNA testing that proved the trial was a mockery of justice."

So much for hoping everyone would get along. Glancing from Dawson to Nelson, Lillie felt like a drop of water on a hot iron.

Dawson pointed his finger at the contractor. "People in this town stood by and allowed an innocent man to go to jail."

Nelson's eyes narrowed. Before he could respond, the door to the inner office suite opened.

General Cameron stood in the doorway, his hand outstretched. "Glad you stopped by early, Karl. We'll have more time to go over the plans for the new museum."

The construction company owner shrugged off his displeasure with Dawson, returned the handshake and followed the general into his inner office.

Once the door closed behind them, Lillie looked at Dawson, willing him to understand she needed to get to work. "You'd better go."

Digging in his pocket, he pulled out Granger's key and dropped it into her hand. "I'll stop by later this afternoon and follow you home after work."

Before she could object, he was gone, leaving her stomach in knots and her nerves stretched thin. She glanced through the window as he hurried along the sidewalk to his car.

Handsome though he was, Lillie needed to realize the special agent was trouble, and right now, she had more than enough to last a lifetime.

FIVE

Leaving post headquarters, Dawson glanced up at the second-story corner suite. In deference to the general, he should have kept his comment about Granger to himself, but he had bristled when the construction tycoon claimed the ex-con had deserved to die.

Dawson had blurted out his objection not just because Granger had been his dad, but because false rhetoric, like idle gossip, could be deadly. Dawson had experienced it firsthand with the hateful words spread around Cotton Grove when he was growing up.

Just like Lillie, Dawson had closed the door to his past. In fact, he had slammed it shut and walked away. Only now Granger's death had cracked it open again.

As he walked past Lillie's car, he thought again of the pretty secretary. High cheekbones. Expressive brows. Emerald eyes that seemed to look beneath the surface and see into the parts of him he closed off from the world. Could she look deep enough to uncover the real person behind the badge?

Did she see a man who wanted to know the truth about his father? Or a man who still harbored ill feelings toward the one person he had needed most when he was growing up?

Sliding behind the wheel of his Camry, Dawson shook his head ever so slightly. As a kid, instead of listening to his mother's constant bashing of his absentee dad, Dawson had created an imaginary bigger-than-life hero.

That false bubble had burst when Granger was convicted of murder. From then on, Dawson had become his own man and no longer held on to the flawed belief that his father loved him. Like folks said, love was overrated. At least that's what Dawson told himself.

Now, with the emotional upheaval rumbling through his gut since he had gotten the call about the shooting, he wasn't sure of how he felt about Granger, and while Lillie was in a completely different class, he didn't know how he felt about her either.

Dawson tried to refocus his attention on the investigation. Instead he kept seeing Lillie, dressed in blood-spattered pajamas and tugging nervously at her silky locks.

Once he arrived at CID headquarters, he poured two cups of coffee and headed for Jamison's office. He needed to brief him on what had happened at the secretary's home and then explain a rather complicated situation that could have bearing on his future.

The sergeant who had recruited Dawson into the military had insisted army entrance forms mirror each recruit's legal birth certificate. If Dawson's mother had failed to provide his father's name, then as far as the sergeant was concerned, Dawson's military paperwork needed to duplicate that same lack of information, even if Dawson had been willing to provide a name.

All of which Dawson would explain to the chief on Monday. Since Jamison was in charge during Wilson's absence, he needed to be brought up to date as well.

"Thanks for taking the call this morning," Jamison said when Dawson handed him the cup of coffee.

"Not a problem."

Jamison took a long slug of the hot brew before asking, "How's the secretary?"

"Back at work."

Raising his brow, Jamison asked, "You okay?"

Dawson nodded. "I'm fine. Just need to get a few things off my chest."

"You've got my attention."

Dawson quickly filled Jamison in on the shooting and the man who had run Lillie off the road. "Her safety's an issue, but she's more concerned about the new Fort Rickman Museum and whether negative publicity about the shooting could impact donations."

"A lot of high rollers will be on post Wednesday along with their checkbooks."

"That's the problem. You've heard of Karl Nelson?"

"As in Nelson Construction Company? He's a local hero. Evidently his father did a lot to foster relations between Fort Rickman and the local community. Once he passed on, Karl took over. Nelson money has put Freemont on the map."

Dawson nodded. "I had a little run-in with Karl this morning."

"Oh?"

"He made a negative comment about Granger." Dawson shrugged. "I set him straight."

The corners of Jamison's mouth twitched. "I'm sure you were respectful and handled the situation with great diplomacy."

"I wanted to jab my finger in his pudgy midriff and tell him to drop and give me fifty push-ups."

Jamison chuckled. "He's probably harmless, but my advice would be to temper your remarks when you're in the general's office."

"Roger that." Dawson downed the rest of his coffee and threw the paper cup in the trash.

"There's something else we need to discuss." He pulled in a deep breath and then explained the tightrope he was walking by investigating a case in which he had a personal interest.

Jamison pursed his lips once Dawson had finished speaking. "I'm not sure what the old man will say on Monday. Wilson likes everything done by the book, but he knows we're down two agents. I was tied up with another case, and anything involving the general's secretary, in my opinion, could become high profile. When the call came in, we needed someone from post to represent the military. You were the only agent available."

Dawson nodded. "Which sounds well and good today, but the chief might see it in a totally different light come Monday."

"I'll take the heat."

Dawson held up his hand. "I don't want you involved, Jamison. This rests on my shoulders."

"But I was the one who assigned you to the case. We'll let the Freemont police handle the investigation while you ensure Ms. Beaumont's safety. If Wilson wants to make a change come Monday, so be it, but until then your job is to keep her safe."

"I want to be up front about everything," Dawson said.

"Which you have been."

"There's one other thing. My father's name was not on my birth certificate. If my relationship to the victim becomes public knowledge, I don't want anyone to think I tried to falsify military records."

"We'll handle that problem when we need to. For right now, focus on security for the general's secretary."

Dawson let out a frustrated breath as he left Jamison's office. He was treading in treacherous waters, especially where Lillie Beaumont was concerned. Keeping her safe meant keeping her under surveillance. Not a difficult task on the surface, but one that could force him to ignore the emotional pull she had on his heart.

Maybe the delay would work to Dawson's advantage. Over the weekend, more facts could come to light. He was probably being overly optimistic, but anything could develop in the next forty-eight hours.

All he had to do was keep Lillie safe until then, but when he returned to her office later that afternoon, the only person he found was the general's aide.

On more than one occasion, Dawson had seen the rather egotistic captain at the club, throwing his weight around and demanding faster service because of his connections with the general. Evidently, the aide didn't realize he had silver bars on his shoulders instead of stars.

"When did Lillie leave?" Dawson asked as he spied her empty desk.

The aide checked his watch. "Probably twenty minutes ago."

"Did she say where she was going?"

"Only that she needed to check on a few things that may have played into the murder."

Dawson's gut tightened. Someone had run Lillie off the road this morning and placed her life in danger. The last thing she needed was to snoop around in a homicide investigation.

To his credit, the captain's face showed the concern he must not have realized earlier. "I…I thought she was meeting you."

"What did she say, exactly?"

"Something about unlocking the answers to what had happened."

Dawson never should have given her the key. More than likely Granger wouldn't have had access to the facilities on post, which Lillie would have realized. She must have driven back to town.

Dawson wasn't sure what he would find in Freemont, but one thing was certain. He had to find Lillie before trouble found her.

Lillie needed to discover what Granger's key unlocked. Confident Dawson planned to follow her home after work, she wanted to distance herself from the CID agent with whom she had already shared too much. She didn't want anyone getting too close, which he seemed to do whenever they were together.

Case in point, she had ended up in his arms this morning. Lulled by his warmth, she had felt secure in his protective embrace. Even the masculine scent of his aftershave played havoc with her normal control. No matter how she reacted emotionally to the CID agent, she didn't need him. She didn't need anyone.

Earlier, she had planned to take a long lunch break to investigate on her own, but with only a few workdays until the big donors would be on post, the last-minute details for the kickoff event for the Fort Rickman Museum required attention.

Lillie had produced a program for the ceremony, which General Cameron needed to review before the end of the workday. She had stayed at her desk throughout the lunch hour to ensure the task was completed on time. She had also contacted the various organizations on post taking part in the special event and asked for a confirmation of the number of people participating.

When she had finally cleared her desk, Lillie bid Captain Banks a hasty goodbye and briefly explained her reason for leaving early. An incoming call captured his attention and allowed her to get away without having to share additional information.

Once in her car, she pulled Granger's key from her pocket. What would it unlock, and what secrets would be revealed about the past? Torn between learning the truth and keeping the past hidden, Lillie jammed it back in her pocket.

Lillie had learned at a young age to protect her heart and had vowed to never allow herself to be vulnerable again. Granger's death forced her to rethink the past, something she hadn't wanted to do.

This morning, she had watched Dawson through her office window as he hustled to his car. *Penny for your thoughts.* The old adage had come to mind when he stopped on the sidewalk and glanced up at the window where she stood.

Surely with the tinted panes he hadn't noticed her staring down at him. Nor had he realized the way her heart tightened in her chest. Before she allowed herself to explore the reason for the internal reaction, she had returned to her desk, intent on focusing on her work instead of the CID agent.

Except here she was hours later, drifting back to his blue eye and blond hair and strong arms that had comforted her this morning.

She shook her head, sending the thought of his strength fleeing, and concentrated instead on the twisting road she needed to follow into town.

Freemont had grown recently with the influx of military to the area. The south side, closest to post, had rapidly spread into an assortment of fly-by-night businesses that catered to soldiers. Used-car dealerships, pawnshops and bars now populated the outskirts of the Georgia town.

A bowling alley and pool hall complex appeared ahead, housed in a prefabricated warehouse that took up most of the block. She found a parking space on the street and, remembering Dawson's warning earlier, locked her doors before she hurried along the sidewalk toward Southside Lanes.

The neon lights inside the building beckoned a welcome that couldn't cover the smell of stale beer and dirty socks. Bowling balls crashed against the lineup of pins, filling the air with the *ding-ding-ding* of the scoreboards. The clerk, mid-thirty-something and as many pounds overweight, stood behind the counter and talked to two guys, who from their buzz haircuts were obviously military.

Lillie stepped into the women's locker room, lifted by a sense of euphoria when she spied a row of lockers along one wall. She tried the key in the various locks, but none opened.

Realizing Granger wouldn't have used the women's locker room, she retraced her steps to the main bowling area. The two military guys had selected their balls and were warming up on a distant lane. The clerk had left the counter unmanned, and the only other patrons were focused on the scoreboard and their games.

Walking quickly, Lillie eased through the open doorway into the men's area and tried the key in the nearby lockers, discouraged when they also failed to open.

Footsteps sounded behind her. Lillie tensed. Her heart hammered in her chest.

"Hey, lady," a deep voice bellowed. "What are you doing?"

Her hands shaking, she dropped the key in her pocket. "I, ah…I thought this was the ladies' room."

Lowering her head, Lillie brushed past the indignant bowler and hurried toward the door, only to walk into the wide body of the clerk.

He grabbed her arm and glared down at her. "What were you doing?"

She tried to wrench free of his grasp. "I…I thought this was the ladies' room."

The other man followed her out. "She was fooling around with the lockers."

The clerk's hold tightened on her arm. "Maybe we should call the cops."

Things were going from bad to worse. "No, please, I was here last week, and I thought I'd left my hairbrush in the locker I used. For some reason, I got mixed up and went in the men's area."

"Open your purse," the clerk demanded.

"What?"

"You heard me. We've had things stolen out of the lockers recently. What did you take?"

Lillie stared indignantly back at the clerk, attempting to appear defiant rather than afraid. Her job. Her reputation. So much was at stake.

"I told you what happened," she insisted.

"And I told you to open your purse."

The man gripped her arm even more tightly, and he pushed her forward toward a small office. "That's it, lady. Maybe you'll be more responsive when you talk to the police."

"Is there a problem?"

Relief buckled her knees as Lillie recognized the voice and turned to see Dawson holding up his CID identification and leveling an intense gaze at the clerk.

"Someone's stealing from our customers. We found this woman in the men's locker room. She refuses to open her purse so I can see if she's taken anything."

"I'm sure there's been a mix-up." Dawson's calm voice appeared to ease the tension in the clerk's stance. "Release her arm, and she'll open her purse." Dawson raised his brow at Lillie.

"Of course I will," she said quickly, relieved when the clerk dropped his hand.

Lillie followed Dawson's suggestion and removed her wallet and a package of tissues so the clerk could view the few items that remained in her handbag.

"As I told you," Lillie said, feeling confident again with Dawson at her side, "I walked into the wrong locker room. My mind was somewhere else."

The clerk didn't seem totally satisfied with her explanation and, once again, Dawson came to her aid.

"A perfectly logical mistake." He smiled at the clerk. "I'll ensure the lady finds her way out. Call Fort Rickman CID if you ever have trouble with military personnel here at the bowling alley."

He slipped his card into the clerk's open hand. "We work closely with the local police. In fact, I was with Sergeant Pritchard this morning. You probably know him."

"Sure." The clerk nodded. "He bowls on Tuesday nights."

Dawson withdrew a twenty-dollar bill from his pocket and offered it to the clerk. "Tell Pritchard the first game's on me. You keep the change."

The man's face brightened. "Will do." He glanced at Lillie. "Sorry for the confusion, ma'am."

"And I apologize for the mix-up."

Dawson took her arm and hurried her toward the door.

"What were you doing?" he asked, his easy demeanor a thing of the past as soon as they stepped outside.

"I told you. I got confused."

"You were checking lockers in the men's room, Lillie. That wasn't smart. When I left this morning, I said I'd be back after work. Why didn't you wait for me?"

"I don't need a bodyguard."

Dawson's eyes focused on a guy slumped behind the wheel of a Chevrolet Suburban parked across the street. She followed his gaze and felt a chill sweep over her.

"A bodyguard is exactly what you need." Dawson continued to stare at the Suburban as the driver started his engine and drove out of sight.

"Was that the same car as this morning?" Lillie asked.

"The only thing I saw was an army sticker on the back bumper."

She shivered. "Just like the car that ran me off the road."

"Which is why you shouldn't be here."

"I need to find out what the key unlocks."

"That's my job, Lillie. Your job is to stay safe."

She shook her head. "I'm going to keep searching."

"You're doing no such thing."

She put her hands on her hips. "You can't tell me what to do. Besides, I don't appreciate being followed."

"I drove into town and saw your car. Easy enough to know you were inside. The bowling alley is on the road from post."

"But you were looking for me."

He shrugged. "I wanted to ensure you didn't get into trouble."

Which had happened when the man at the bowling alley grabbed her arm.

Dawson raised his brow and stared down at her, making her skin tingle. "The way I see it, Lillie, you need to do two things. Number one: go home. Number two: don't get involved."

"Those both entail getting me out of the picture, and that's not happening. There's an option you haven't mentioned."

"What's that?"

"We work together." She shrugged. "If not, we'll say goodbye here."

"You're being headstrong and foolish."

She straightened her spine and leveled him with a confrontational glare. "People have said many things about me, but I won't give up or give in. A man died this morning before he could tell me something about my mother. I have to find out what he wanted me to know."

"You're putting your life in danger."

She nodded. "If so, then I do need a bodyguard." Before she could stop herself, she quirked her brow. "You seem to be volunteering for the job."

Dawson was as determined as she was and had left her no choice but to suggest they team up. Hopefully, she wouldn't regret making the offer.

Then looking into Dawson's blue eyes, which sparkled with an audacity that matched her own eyes, she realized the CID agent kept showing up when she was most in need. Surely it was only a coincidence. She shouldn't worry, but Dawson's father was an ex-con. Maybe the handsome CID agent had secrets of his own. Secrets involving her mother's death and what had happened long ago or secrets about what had caused a man to be murdered on her front porch this morning.

Either way, Dawson was the last person she should be working with yet, at the present moment, she had nowhere else to turn. She needed answers that perhaps only he could provide.

SIX

Dawson kept Lillie's Honda in sight as he followed her across town to a small gym that smelled like floor mats and sweat. A few lockers stood against the wall in the common area. Lillie tried the key but with no success, and before anyone noticed them milling about, Dawson escorted her back to her car.

"The main workout center is on the other side of town." He opened her car door. "Follow me. If there's a problem, flash your lights."

The scent of her perfume wafted past him and made him want to step closer and breathe more deeply. Her dark lashes fluttered over her cheeks, and her lips parted ever so slightly as if she wanted to say something. Maybe that she appreciated his help.

All too quickly, the moment passed. She slid behind the wheel and nodded for him to close the door.

Dawson would let her pretend to be Miss Independent, but he'd seen behind her strong facade this morning when she sat huddled on the couch in her living room.

Traffic in town was light, and Lillie followed close behind him as they headed to the newer facility. Parking next to the gym, he noticed the Fort Rickman stickers on a number of the cars in the lot.

"Must be a popular place," Dawson said as Lillie joined him on the sidewalk.

"You're not a member?"

He smiled. "I use the gym on post."

When they stepped inside, Dawson was impressed by the rows of treadmills and elliptical machines, the rack of weights and other bodybuilding equipment available to the members. Maybe the state-of-the-art facility was worth the hefty membership and monthly fees.

The locker rooms were on opposite ends of the central workout area. A number of men looked up as Lillie headed toward the ladies' room. Dawson kept watch to ensure no one bothered her.

He didn't have long to wait and was relieved when she reappeared. Lillie shook her head and dropped the key into his hand. "Only a few of the lockers were in use. No luck with the key."

Dawson found the same thing in the men's changing area. The entire trip seemed a waste of time until they headed for the parking lot and spied Captain Mark Banks digging in the backseat of his BMW. Standing next to the general's aide was a big, burly guy with a shaved head and massive biceps.

Mark pulled out a workout bag and slammed the door before he noticed Dawson and Lillie. He swaggered toward them, smiling. "You two don't look like you're dressed for working out."

"Just wanted to check out the equipment." Dawson flicked his gaze over the expensive Beemer. "Seems like a top-of-the-line facility."

"Tom Reynolds runs the place." Mark pointed his thumb to his beefy friend, probably early forties, and introduced Dawson and Lillie. "Tom keeps the equipment running like clockwork. Ten times better than what we have on post."

Dawson extended his hand. The beef had a killer grip.

"Good to meet you." Tom flicked his gaze to Lillie. "Ma'am."

"Do you also manage the smaller gym on the other side of town?" she asked.

Tom shook his head. "That's a private operation. Karl Nelson brought in this franchise. I've been the manager for the last five years."

"Invite Tom to post to advise our gym director on how to upgrade," Dawson told the aide.

Mark nodded. "Remind me on Monday, Lillie. I'll run it by General Cameron."

The look on his face confirmed what Dawson already knew. The general's aide was interested in Lillie. She probably hadn't noticed.

Tom Reynolds dug in his pocket and pulled out two small cards. "Here're a couple free passes good for a week of workouts. See if you like what we've got to offer."

"Will do. Thanks."

"You two stay safe." Mark smiled at Lillie as both men headed toward the front entrance.

Dawson pointed her toward their cars. "Something about that guy bothers me."

She shrugged off his comment. "Mark's nice enough, although he sometimes thinks he's the man in charge instead of General Cameron."

Maybe Dawson didn't have to worry about Lillie, after all. As pretty as she was, working in the same office with the general's secretary could take a man off track, which is what Dawson needed to ensure didn't happen to him.

"Where to next?" he asked.

"There's a bus station downtown."

"You lead the way this time."

They parked on a side street in the older section of Freemont. A number of buildings sat abandoned, and the few businesses still in operation looked as if they were hanging on by a thread.

The sun sat low in the sky, casting long shadows over the abandoned storefronts and sagging facades badly in need of repair. His eyes searched the area for anything that spelled danger.

"Stay by my side." His right hand flexed closer to his hip, aware of the weight of his weapon. He didn't want anything to happen, but he was prepared in case something did occur. "Maybe you should have remained in the car."

"You've been watching too much television, Dawson. This is Freemont, Georgia." Then, as if realizing her error, she raised her hand to her throat. "I almost said nothing happens in this small town."

He touched her elbow. "You don't have to do this if it's too difficult."

"Yes, I do."

The bus station had a musty smell, as if rising water from the nearby river had at some point flooded the aged structure. Fluorescent lights cast the terminal in an artificial glow that made Lillie's face look paler than usual. Wide-eyed, she glanced at the row of lockers on the back wall.

A clerk, wearing a cardigan sweater and bow tie, stood behind the counter. Two men were slumped in chairs, chins on their chests. Threadbare jackets and well-worn shoes screamed "down on their luck." A woman with platinum hair and too-bright lipstick sat with her arm around a little boy, not more than eight or nine, who fiddled with a small electronic device he held in his hands. She gazed at Lillie and Dawson with tired eyes and then checked her watch. A fourth patron sat on a far bench, his face obscured by the newspaper he was reading.

The clerk raised his brow, but before he said anything, a bus braked to a stop at the side of the building. The driver stepped through the double glass doors. "Got any passengers for me, Harry?"

The clerk nodded in his direction before announcing, "The six p.m. bus to Atlanta is now ready to board."

Taking up his post at the door, he prepared to collect the tickets as the four adults and one child slowly gathered their belongings and lumbered forward.

Dawson motioned Lillie toward the lockers where, once again, she tried the key. Glancing over his shoulder, Dawson watched the blonde woman hug the little boy, who was apparently traveling on his own. The clerk waited as she gave the boy final instructions to sit behind the driver and to call Mama when he arrived at his destination.

Turning back, Dawson pointed to a locker on the bottom row. "Try that one."

Lillie inserted the key. The lock clicked open. She glanced up at Dawson and smiled.

Both of them bent down and stared into the compartment, big enough for a suitcase. Dawson's elation plummeted, seeing the empty space.

"Only bus patrons are allowed to use the lockers."

Dawson bristled at the sound of the clerk's voice. He didn't want to show his CID identification and raise the clerk's suspicions or have him call the local authorities. Some of the good old boys on the force didn't cotton to sharing information with the military. Pritchard had seemed guarded this morning, and although Dawson planned to notify the police if they found anything, he wanted the CID to have the first look at evidence they uncovered.

The man moved closer.

Lillie closed the locker and stood. She handed the key to the clerk. "My uncle bused in from Atlanta last week. He has a memory problem. We're worried it might be the start of Alzheimer's. He was sure he had left something in the locker, but it was empty."

The clerk's frown faded. "I understand completely. We're just glad your uncle used our bus service. Anything I can do for you, just let me know."

"You've been most helpful." Lillie placed her hand on Dawson's arm and turned her sweet face toward him. "Well, dear, we need to get home for dinner."

Dawson steered Lillie toward the door. The sun had set, and darkness covered the area by the time they stepped into the chilly night air. Neither of them spoke until they neared their cars.

"I'm sorry we didn't find anything," he said, patting her soft hand.

She smiled before she opened her fist. Even in the half-light from the lone streetlight, he could see the small flash drive.

"Good job," he wanted to say, but when he looked up he saw an SUV with tinted windows parked in an abandoned lot across the street.

"Get in your car, Lillie. Lock your doors and drive back to post headquarters. I'll question the guy in the car and keep him here. As soon as I'm satisfied he's not a threat, I'll follow you to post."

She started to hesitate.

"Now."

Dawson kept his eyes trained on the Suburban as he crossed the street, relieved when Lillie's headlights disappeared from sight. Before he could get close enough to the parked vehicle, the engine purred to life, tires screeched and the SUV raced away in the opposite direction from post.

Dawson had made a mistake thinking he could detain the driver, but at least the SUV was headed away from Lillie.

Once again, he saw the military decal on the rear bumper. Only this time he saw the license plate as well.

Raising his cell, he hit speed dial for CID headquarters. Corporal Otis answered. Dawson relayed the number. "Find out who owns the vehicle."

"Roger that, sir."

"And get back to me ASAP."

Darkness settled in around Lillie's car as she headed along the winding road that led to Fort Rickman. Overhead, tree limbs swayed in the night. The temperature had dropped. She turned up the heater and adjusted the vent, but even with the warm air blowing over her, she still felt cold.

Glancing at the rearview mirror, she saw approaching headlights. Her heart pounded, and her throat went dry, remembering the light-colored Suburban. The same man who had come after her earlier today could be barreling down on her once again.

She pushed on the accelerator, determined to stay well ahead of the vehicle. It had big, boxy headlights elevated well off the ground that marked it as an SUV.

Lillie glanced at her cell phone in the passenger seat, wondering whether to call Dawson and tell him she needed help.

Another, more frightening, thought circled through her mind. Dawson kept talking about Lillie being in danger. What if the man who had killed Granger had come after his son?

A queasy feeling settled in the pit of her stomach. She pulled her left hand from the wheel and rubbed it over her abdomen, hoping to quell the upset.

Her heart lurched again when she saw the lights nearing even as she increased her speed.

She pressed down on the accelerator, willing her car to go faster. At any moment, she expected to feel the huge sports vehicle crash into her rear fender and send her swerving off the road.

Her hands gripped the wheel.

A cry escaped her lips.

Her phone rang, but she ignored the sound and focused totally on the road.

An intersection loomed ahead. She had no choice but to keep moving forward.

"Please, God." She prayed no one would be approaching from the other direction.

The trill of her phone continued to fill the car. The reflection from the headlights blinded her. Her heart exploded in her chest.

She charged through the intersection, expecting to be hit either from the rear or by some unknown driver approaching on the side road.

In the blink of an eye, the SUV was gone.

A rush of nausea swept over her. Her head pounded with delayed tension, and tears of relief and confusion clouded her vision. She blinked them back, trying to determine what had happened.

Before she could put the pieces together, she saw another set of headlights not far behind her. Once again her cell rang.

She pushed the phone to her ear.

"Lillie?" Dawson's voice. "I'm right behind you. You're safe. Ease up on the gas and pull to the side of the road."

"But—"

"You're okay, Lillie. The Suburban turned at the intersection."

Still unsure of what had happened, Lillie decelerated and angled off the road. She kept the engine running and her foot poised on the accelerator until she saw Dawson step from his car.

"I lost the guy in town," he said as she stumbled onto the

pavement. "He was headed north, away from post. Evidently he circled around and caught up to you."

Dawson stood in the glare of the headlights, big and protecting. Once again, he had saved her.

She felt dizzy with the rush of emotions. Suddenly she didn't know whether to cry or laugh so she did both, causing Dawson's eyes to widen and his arms to reach for her.

Lillie's knees weakened, and for one glorious moment, she fell into his outstretched arms. Her heart beat against his and the fear left her, replaced with another feeling that caused her to be equally as emotional. Tears overflowed her eyes and cascaded down her cheeks, tears of gratitude that Dawson had arrived in time.

She'd been alone for so long and had never thought she needed or wanted anyone else in her life. At this moment, she realized her desire to go through life alone might have been a mistake.

SEVEN

Dawson didn't want Lillie to leave his arms, but they were on a lonely stretch of back road and exposed both to the dropping temperature and to anyone who might be watching and waiting in the night.

"Let's get back to Fort Rickman." He looked into her tearstained face. "You'll be safe on post."

He had given her his handkerchief earlier. Now he wiped her tears with his fingertips, wanting to touch her cheeks and trail his hands through her hair.

Holding himself in check, he gave her an encouraging hug before he walked her to her car. "Can you drive?"

She nodded and sniffed and tried to smile at him with that determined expression she used to cover her own insecurity.

"I'll follow close behind you. I don't think he'll come back tonight."

"If it hadn't been for you—"

"The Suburban turned off the road and raced away, Lillie. That's what you need to keep in mind. Besides, I never should have let you leave the bus station alone."

"No, Dawson. I...I owe you my—"

"You don't owe me anything. Now get behind the wheel, and we'll meet up at your office. My cell phone will be on."

She nodded and tried to appear strong, but Dawson was

worried. Lillie had to be exhausted and in shock from the string of incidents that had happened, one after the other.

He planned to call Pritchard in the morning and fill him in, but first he needed to see what was on the flash drive—information Granger's killer or killers didn't want brought to light?

Dawson followed Lillie while he flicked his gaze back and forth, searching the surrounding area. Thankfully, they only passed a few cars along the way. He sighed with relief when both he and Lillie passed through the main gate and headed toward her office.

Once parked, they walked along the sidewalk and up the stairs together. Dawson's attention was on the darkness and anyone who might be hiding in the shadows. Although it was doubtful the elusive Suburban had gained access to post, Dawson wouldn't let down his guard.

Lillie had a master key to the main door. The staff duty noncommissioned officer, Howard Murphy—a sergeant with a square face and serious eyes—met them in the hallway. Lillie introduced Dawson and made an excuse about needing to catch up on some work, which the NCO seemed to accept, before she led Dawson upstairs to the general's suite.

Once there, she shrugged out of her coat and hung it on a rack. "I could make coffee."

He nodded. "That's probably a good idea."

The smell of the rich roasted beans filled the office as he took off his coat and loosened his tie. Even without caffeine, he knew he would spend another sleepless night. At least until he was sure Lillie was safe. Maybe then he'd be able to relax.

"Cream or sugar?"

"Neither, thanks."

She poured the coffee and handed him a mug. He took a long swig of the hot brew and watched as she stirred sweetener and two packets of creamer into her own cup. Since they had entered post headquarters, Lillie had seemed more composed, as if she had stepped back into the role of the very competent administrative assistant to the commanding general.

Whether she was totally in control or showing her emotions, Dawson wasn't sure which side of Lillie he liked better. Certainly he didn't want fear to be the reason she allowed him to see behind her tough facade, but if truth be told, he was drawn to the woman who exposed her feelings. As much as he tried to focus on the investigation, he would never forget the way she felt in his arms.

Dawson couldn't think about that. Not now. Not when she was looking at him and waiting for him to tell her what they should do next.

He motioned her toward her computer. "Let's see what's on that flash drive."

Lillie sat in her desk chair and slipped the small memory device into the USB port. She opened the file that popped up.

Dawson leaned over her shoulder. He drew closer, inhaling her perfume and enjoying the feel of his arm against hers.

As he watched, Granger's face appeared on the screen. Dawson had only seen photographs of his father while he was still alive. Now he stared at the angular jaw, gray hair and wrinkled face, hardened by the elements from years of working construction.

The ex-convict's eyes were guarded and cautious. He glanced over his shoulder as if to ensure he was alone.

"My name is Granger Ford. I've uncovered information about a number of crimes that occurred twenty-five years ago. Hopefully, what I've found will eventually lead to Irene Beaumont's killer. I loaded the information into a jump drive and hid it in the locker at the bus depot. If you're watching this, you found the memory device. More information needs to be uncovered so Irene's killer can be arrested and brought to justice."

Granger's deep voice sounded from the speakers. The same voice Dawson had heard over the phone just a few nights earlier—a voice and a request to meet, both of which Dawson had rejected.

A weight hung heavily over his shoulders. He knew he had made a terrible error. Granger had wanted to share information with his son. If Dawson had put his personal feelings aside, his father might still be alive. Instead Granger had turned to Lillie for help, hoping she would continue the search for Irene Beaumont's killer.

Now, leaning close to her, Dawson knew he couldn't let his personal struggle with his father cloud his ability to be an effective agent. He also had to ensure his desire to protect Lillie didn't get in the way of uncovering the truth. Somehow her mother's death played into his father's murder.

Right now, Dawson needed answers, yet the lives both he and Lillie had created for themselves could be destroyed in the process. If the investigation uncovered too many secrets from the past, she could lose her job on post. Similarly, Dawson's chance for promotion might end once the truth about his father came to light. The stakes were high, and they needed to move forward carefully.

Would either of them be hurt as the truth was revealed? Only time would tell. And right now, Dawson and Lillie were running out of time.

Lillie stared at the computer screen, seeing the man who had pounded on her door less than twenty-four hours earlier. Sitting at her desk with Dawson hanging over her shoulder caused her neck to tingle with a mix of apprehension and attraction. Although tired, she was also on edge and anxious to hear what the video would reveal.

Granger seemed equally anxious and glanced repeatedly to where a cheap reproduction of an oil painting hung askew over a double bed.

Lillie recognized the bedspread. "He's at the Hi-Way Motel."

Dawson nodded. "You're right." His breath fanned her cheek. She forced herself to concentrate on the monitor.

"Someone knows I'm getting close to learning what happened to Irene Beaumont," Granger said on the screen. "If I'm killed, I hope whoever has these files will continue to investigate on their own."

With a drawl, Granger laid out the backstory. Slowly, methodically, he talked about the jobs he had picked up working construction in various towns around the South, including the times he had been employed by Nelson Construction.

"On-site, the guys were tight-lipped," he said from the video. "After work, with a few beers under their belts, they talked. Property theft was a fact of life. Everyone knew the steel drum had been stolen. Probably from Nelson's company."

Lillie pulled in a sharp breath when he mentioned a woman's body found near the river.

"Irene Beaumont had left Freemont years earlier and had abandoned her little girl," Granger continued. "Although I kept my opinions to myself, I felt the woman had been wrongly judged by the entire town."

Lillie scooted her chair back as if to distance herself from Granger's statements, but the video continued to play.

"At the time, I wondered why the police hadn't made more of an effort to find Ms. Beaumont instead of writing her off as a bad mother who wanted nothing to do with her daughter."

Granger sucked air through his thin lips. "I had been working for a few weeks on a short-term project with Nelson Construction when she initially went missing, but I moved on to another area of the state after that job ended. When I returned to Freemont ten years later, I never suspected the police would come after me."

Dawson leaned in closer.

"At the time, I was staying at the Hi-Way Motel. They ransacked my room and found Mrs. Beaumont's picture stuffed under the mattress."

Lillie turned from the monitor.

Dawson touched her arm. "We can stop the video if it's too difficult to watch."

She shook her head and slipped from her chair. Wrapping her arms across her chest, she walked to the window and stared out into the night, wanting to clear her mind.

Dawson approached her. She could see his reflection in the window. Eyes wide, brow raised, he lifted his hand to her shoulder. The tenderness of his touch eased her internal struggle. She swallowed down the lump of confusion and regret that had threatened to suffocate her only moments earlier.

"I'm being foolish, Dawson. We need to know what's on the video. All of it."

"I can watch and tell you what Granger said."

She shook her head. "No, she was my mother. I need to hear everything."

"Maybe tomorrow, Lillie."

She turned to face him, never expecting his concern to be such a powerful draw. She wanted to move even closer and rest her head on his shoulder and allow his arms to encircle her.

Granger's voice drawled on from the computer, but her

focus was on Dawson's eyes and the depth of his own struggle that reached out to her like a lifeline.

"We're in this together, Lillie," he said. She wanted to believe Dawson, but right now she wasn't sure of anything, especially when it involved a CID agent whose father had been accused of murdering her mom.

Dawson might be grieving, but he was still a cop. Would he remain an ally or would he turn on her and close her out just as the voice from her mother's bedroom—a voice she would never forget—had done that night so long ago?

She glanced at the monitor. "Granger's still talking." Dawson hesitated a long moment before he stepped aside.

Lillie pulled in a determined breath. Returning to her desk, she slipped back into her chair, but she kept her eyes on the computer screen instead of the CID special agent next to her. They might be in this together, but they were coming from opposite directions.

Dawson was looking for clues and evidence and bits and pieces of two murders that were joined over time. Lillie felt like a bystander, watching a drama unfold that was pulling her into the action when all she wanted was to return to the safe and solitary life she had known.

Before Granger had knocked on her door.

Before the bullet had taken his life.

Before Dawson had stepped into her controlled existence with his broad shoulders and blue eyes that saw more than she wanted to reveal.

If she went back to the way life had been, she would be alone again. Dawson wouldn't be there, and at the moment, she wasn't ready to lose him. Someday, in the not too distant future, their paths would part. No telling how she would feel when they said goodbye.

All she knew was at this moment she needed someone at her side. Someone willing to walk with her into the darkness and discover the truth—no matter how twisted it would be—about her past.

At this moment, she needed Dawson.

Dawson watched the video as Granger explained about his trial and the defense attorney who'd seemed less interested in what his client had to say and more interested in copping a plea. To his credit, Granger had refused to plead, knowing nothing could be gained by admitting guilt when he was innocent.

Easy enough to read the writing on the wall, Granger mused on the tape, his face drawn. "The prosecution needed someone to pin the murder on, and I had a bull's-eye painted on my back."

When the video stopped, Dawson turned to Lillie, concerned about her well-being. "It's getting late. Why don't you take a break?"

"We have two more files to open, but a cool drink of water sounds good. There's a small refrigerator near the conference room."

Dawson followed her down the hall and paused beside a table on which a model of the new Fort Rickman Museum was displayed. The three-story structure was surrounded by large cement flowerpots and shade trees. A path headed toward the nearby river where benches provided picnic areas for visitors to enjoy after touring the facility.

He whistled under his breath. "The layout's pretty impressive."

"Karl Nelson used an Atlanta architect who's well thought of in the South." Lillie reached into the refrigerator.

"Maybe I should have cut him a little slack this morning."

She smiled. "He and his father have done a lot of good. Burl Nelson's memory is revered because of the work he did to ensure Fort Rickman remained open when many posts were forced to close. Without the military, Freemont would go back to being a sleepy little farm town."

Lillie handed a bottle of water to Dawson. "Karl has funded a lot of businesses in town and helped a number of folks. After my mother's body was found, he stopped by my foster parents' house, visibly upset that the steel drum had been from his own construction company, even though everyone knew it had been stolen. My foster parents were good people, but they didn't have anything extra. Karl insisted on paying my tuition and books at a small college not far from Freemont."

No doubt about it, Dawson had misjudged the construction mogul.

"When it came time to find a job," she continued, "he made a few phone calls. I had to go through the application process, but I was eventually offered a position on post."

"And worked your way up to the top."

She shrugged. "It's a respected job with good benefits, which I want to keep."

Dawson understood the deeper meaning to her statement. Lillie didn't want anything about Granger's death and the investigation to tarnish her standing with the general or the civil service administration that had hired her. He glanced down at the museum model, knowing she didn't want anything to affect the building project either.

Water bottles in hand, they returned to her desk. The next file they opened was a text document that contained three women's names.

"Somehow the women must tie in with what Granger found." Dawson wished he had more information.

Lillie opened the last file.

Granger's face reappeared. "With long hours to kill in prison, guys talk, sometimes more than they should."

Dawson's inner radar told him to pay attention. He leaned closer to the screen.

"A guy named Leonard Simpson told me his dad owned a bar in Atlanta. Some college kid got drunk one night over the Martin Luther King weekend and talked about three prostitutes his brother had killed."

Lillie's eyes widened. Her hand flew to her mouth.

"The women in the previous file," Dawson said, making the connection.

"The college kid claimed their bodies would never be found," Granger said on the video.

Dawson's gut tightened.

"They would never be found," the ex-con repeated. "Because the three women had been placed in steel drums and buried underground."

EIGHT

Dawson and Lillie searched the internet to find more information about the three women listed on Granger's flash drive, but without success. Lillie was unable to hide her fatigue. Dawson encouraged her to relax on the couch and close her eyes.

Glancing up from the computer, he was relieved when she finally fell asleep. Rising from the desk chair, he reached for a throw that lay on the opposite end of the couch. Opening the plush velour, he covered her arms and legs and smiled as she cuddled into the warmth of the blanket.

Hopefully she'd get some much-needed rest. Returning to the computer, he accessed his own email and opened the attachment from Pritchard that contained the picture of Billy Everett. After printing the photo, he logged in to the archives of the Atlanta newspaper and searched for information about the women. Eventually, he located three short fillers on their disappearances, noting the dates the women had last been seen were in consecutive years, all in January.

Wondering if the dates were significant, Dawson plugged them into the search engine. The answer popped onto the screen. The dates coincided with the Martin Luther King Jr. holiday in each of the three years.

What Dawson needed now was something that tied the

Atlanta women to Irene Beaumont. The muscles in his neck tensed as he read story after story. He flexed his shoulders and, once again, glanced at Lillie, relieved she was able to rest. Morning would come soon enough. Hopefully by then Dawson would know where to turn next.

Refocusing on the archives, he eventually found a short piece buried in the Metro section. The article made note of the three Atlanta women who had disappeared in different years, but each over the Martin Luther King holiday. Jessica Baxter, the reporter who penned the story, dubbed the three women the "MLK Missing Women."

Because the women were prostitutes, the journalist claimed their disappearances had seemingly gone unnoticed. Homicides were commonplace in Atlanta. Dawson knew the reality of police investigation in a big city and the large number of crimes that went unsolved.

Stepping into the hallway so as not to wake Lillie, he called the Atlanta prison to ensure Leonard Simpson, the convict Granger had mentioned, was still behind bars. Once confirmed, Dawson made arrangements to interrogate Simpson the following day.

His next call was to CID headquarters to check on the Suburban's license plate, which turned out to have been stolen. Whoever was after Lillie knew enough to cover his tracks. Eventually, the guy who had come after Lillie would make a mistake.

Dawson's third call was to the Atlanta police department. After all these years, he doubted anyone would remember the three women who had gone missing, but as the saying went, nothing ventured, nothing gained.

The police sergeant who answered his inquiry seemed less than willing to search through the files of missing women. He sighed over the phone when Dawson pressed the issue. "Do you know how many missing-persons cases are reported in Atlanta each year?"

Dawson got the message. He thanked the sergeant for his time and, on a hunch, called the Atlanta newspaper. The night-shift reporter who answered was more accommodating than the cop, but what he told Dawson was equally frustrating. Jessica Baxter had retired from the paper five years earlier.

Dawson was batting zero. "Any chance you could contact Ms. Baxter? Tell her the Criminal Investigation Division at Fort Rickman is interested in information about the MLK Missing Women." He provided his name and cell number, but feared the message would never be relayed and would prove to be another dead end.

Discouraged, Dawson returned to Lillie's office and stared out the window, wondering what the new day would bring. Hopefully, Leonard Simpson would confirm the story Granger had provided. A lot of years had passed, and the trail of the missing women could be not only cold, but completely obscured by time.

While Lillie slept, Dawson retrieved his gym bag and a change of clothes he kept in his car and used the shower facilities outside the duty NCO's office. Dawson accepted a box of doughnuts from Sergeant Murphy.

Returning to Lillie's office, Dawson perked a fresh pot of coffee. As he drank the first cup, he couldn't keep his eyes off Lillie's sweet face. Her beauty was more than surface. Over the past twenty-four hours, he had seen glimpses of the inner strength and courage that made him admire not only her beauty but also her resolve to learn more about her past. Yet that determination could also get her in trouble if she charged into areas that were outside her realm of expertise. For her own safety, Lillie needed to leave the investigation to him.

As first light of dawn warmed the distant sky, Dawson touched her shoulder. Her eyes flew open.

"You fell asleep." He smiled at the mix of emotions that played over her face, first confusion, then recognition, then embarrassment as she pushed aside the throw and pulled herself up to a sitting position.

She raked her fingers through her hair in an attempt to adjust the wayward strands into a semblance of order. The beguiling locks invited his touch. He stepped back to ensure he didn't succumb to the temptation.

"You should have awakened me earlier," she said. "I closed my eyes for a moment, never expecting to sleep all night."

"You were exhausted." He handed her a filled mug. "See how you like my coffee."

She took a sip and smiled. "Perfect."

Dawson pointed to the box of doughnuts. "Sergeant Murphy stopped by the bakery this morning and brought back breakfast."

"Did he ask what we were working on all night?"

"I told him you were on a deadline for a project the general wanted."

She raised her brow. "Stretching the truth?"

"Isn't the general interested in getting to the bottom of Granger's murder?"

"Yes, of course."

"Well, so are we."

Lillie tilted her head. "You changed clothes?"

He nodded. "And showered downstairs."

"Were you on the internet the rest of the night?"

He shrugged. "I closed my eyes for a few minutes."

"I think you're stretching the truth just as you did with Sergeant Murphy." Lillie glanced at her computer. "Did you find anything new?"

"The significance of the mid-January disappearances. Each of the three Atlanta women disappeared over the Martin Luther King holiday."

Lillie's eyes grew wide. "The kid who claimed his brother buried women in steel drums talked to the bar owner over the MLK weekend."

"That's right." Dawson handed her Jessica Baxter's article. "I also found this."

Lillie quickly read the piece. "Call the newspaper and talk to the reporter. She might have more information."

Dawson almost smiled at her enthusiasm. "I already did. Unfortunately, Ms. Baxter retired from journalism a number of years ago. The guy I talked to said he'd pass on my message, but I'm not holding my breath."

He handed Lillie the picture of Billy Everett. "Does he look familiar?"

She shook her head. "Growing up, I didn't know many people in Freemont. My foster parents lived in the country. After my mother's body was unearthed, I was home-schooled."

"What about the missing Atlanta women? Anything familiar about their names?"

"Nothing comes to mind. Do you think their disappearances have bearing on my mother's death?"

"Granger made note of their names, so he must have thought there was a connection. I plan to drive to Atlanta today and talk to the convict."

"Leonard Simpson, the man Granger knew?"

"That's right. I want to hear the story from his own lips and then track down his father. Hopefully he might be able to provide more information."

"Which could lead to my mother's killer?"

"You said you were born in Atlanta, Lillie. Maybe the killer knew her there and followed her to Freemont."

Her face clouded. "Are you sure you're not making too much of a leap between what happened to my mother and the three women who disappeared in Atlanta?"

"What else do we have to go on?"

She placed the mug on the table and rubbed her hands over her arms. "How's Billy Everett play into the picture?"

Dawson shrugged. "The motel clerk saw him hanging around town. Granger was looking for information about your mother's murder. He could have contacted Everett."

Lillie nodded. "And Everett could have told the killer that Granger was snooping around."

"It's hard to know what's relevant, but the important thing right now is to keep you safe. You need some place to stay while I'm out of town. Do you have a girlfriend you could visit?"

She shook her head.

"What about your foster parents?"

"They live in the country and are getting on in years. I don't want them brought into the situation."

"They love you, Lillie."

"And I love them, which is exactly why I want them kept out of this. Besides, I'm going with you to Atlanta."

"No way."

"I'm as involved as you are, Dawson, maybe more so."

"A prison's not the place for a woman."

"Then I'll wait outside in the car."

"You're staying in Freemont."

"I'll follow you to Atlanta. You can't stop me."

Working on her own, Lillie could get into a lot of trouble, especially with someone on the loose who wanted to do her harm.

Keeping Lillie close was the only way Dawson knew to keep her safe, and the most important job was doing just that.

* * *

Sitting next to Dawson in the passenger seat, Lillie realized she might have made a mistake to insist on going with him to Atlanta. He hadn't wanted her to tag along, but she wanted access to the information he might not otherwise share with her. She seemed to be the only one insisting they were in this investigation together. Dawson was always encouraging her to stay safe while he put the pieces of the puzzle together.

Leaving Freemont, they had stopped at her house so she could change out of her slept-in clothes from yesterday. Once on the highway, Dawson remained silent, as if focusing on something other than the headstrong woman sitting next to him.

Lillie watched the mile markers tick off their progress. By midmorning, they had accessed the connector into the heart of the downtown area and, after a series of turns, pulled into the parking lot at the state prison.

Looking through the car window, Lillie sucked in a shaky breath, feeling intimidated by the huge stone structure. Entering the building seemed even more threatening.

After Dawson signed them in, two prison guards escorted them through a maze of security checks. Sliding steel doors opened, allowing them access into a series of protective barriers, and then clanged shut behind them as they headed deeper and deeper into the interior of the confinement facility.

Lillie's neck tingled with apprehension. She glanced at Dawson, who must have been aware of her unease. He placed his hand on the small of her back and drew her ever so slightly closer as their footfalls echoed down the long, tiled corridor.

Finally seated at an interrogation table, they watched as

Leonard Simpson, in his late forties with a receding hairline and pasty complexion, was ushered into the room.

After introducing himself and explaining he was on official CID business, Dawson asked the convict a number of questions about how he had known Granger Ford and the various topics they had talked about while incarcerated.

Eventually Dawson wove his way to the reason for their visit. "Granger said your father owned a bar in Atlanta and mentioned a bizarre story that involved three Atlanta women and steel drums."

A spark of interest flashed from the convict's eyes. "The drunken college kid who spilled his guts one night about the three prostitutes."

Leonard shook his head as if even he couldn't believe the kid's stupidity. "Everyone thinks a guy that goes to college is supersmart. That's what Granger thought. Always talking about his own kid who got a degree through the military."

A muscle in Dawson's jaw twitched.

"I got tired of hearing about what a good kid he was and how proud Granger was of him." Simpson glanced at Lillie. "You know what I mean?"

"What…what else did he say about his son?" Lillie asked.

"Granger's former girlfriend didn't let him contact his son. Some kind of deal they made. It ate at him. Probably why Granger talked about the kid so much. Especially after he got involved with the Christian prison ministry." Leonard sniffed and eyed Lillie. "You know how people are after they get religion. They want everyone to know about the mistakes they've made. How they need to do something good to make it up to the person they hurt."

Lillie glanced at Dawson. She could see the tension in his neck and the way his fingers gripped the edge of the table.

"How had Granger hurt his son?" she asked.

"Not being there for the kid. Granger said the Lord had

forgiven him, but he needed to beg forgiveness from his son as well." Simpson flicked dust off the table and stretched back in the chair. "Fact was, Granger believed what the chaplain told him about God's love and mercy. When his case was overturned, Granger was sure God had given him a second chance. Said he was going to find the real killer so his son would know the truth."

Dawson let out a ragged breath and then leaned across the table. "Let's go back to the college kid in the bar. What did he tell your father that night?"

"That his brother killed three hookers and buried them in steel drums." Simpson pursed his lips. "Upset my dad real bad. He didn't know what to do."

Dawson continued the questioning until, seemingly satisfied with the information, he finally asked, "Did your father ever see the college kid again?"

"You'd have to ask him."

"Which is exactly what I plan to do."

Leonard provided his parents' address before the prison guard prepared to escort him back to his cell.

The convict sniffed, his eyes on Lillie. "If…if you see my parents, tell them I'm okay."

"Maybe you should consider talking to the chaplain," she offered. "The lessons Granger learned about love and mercy are for all God's children."

Simpson narrowed his gaze. "Just tell my mama to keep praying for me."

Dawson remained silent as they left the prison grounds. Lillie knew he was probably thinking about his father. He needed time to process what he had heard, especially about Granger being proud of Dawson.

"I could use a cup of coffee," he finally admitted as they headed through the downtown section of Atlanta.

She spied a colorful awning in the distance. "There's a coffee shop in the upcoming block on the right."

They parked on the street. Once inside, Dawson pointed her toward a table by the window while he stood in line to place their order.

Lillie glanced at the stream of traffic outside, noting a number of light-colored SUVs with tinted windows. Although she should have felt safe, she couldn't shake the anxiety that had wrapped around her ever since entering the prison.

A few Saturday shoppers walked along the sidewalk, carrying purchases in plastic bags. None of them seemed the least bit threatening, yet Lillie couldn't overcome the feeling that someone was watching her.

She drummed her fingers on the table and tried to think of something—anything—except three Atlanta women who had been murdered long ago.

A car horn blew. She looked up in time to see a white SUV swerve away from the curb and into the flow of traffic. Her heart lurched when she noticed the army decal on the rear bumper, exactly where the decal had been on the sport-utility vehicle that ran her off the road.

Her neck tingled. She flicked her gaze back to where Dawson stood waiting in the long line.

A man bumped into her table as he walked past. She couldn't see his face, but she did see the backpack strapped over his shoulders and his unkempt red hair. Billy Everett's picture came to mind.

Before she could get Dawson's attention, the guy had left the coffee shop and disappeared into a throng of people passing by. Surely the redhead hadn't followed them to Atlanta.

Once again, she looked at the street where three teenage boys huddled together on the sidewalk. One of them, a muscular kid with baggy pants that hung from his hips, pointed to her through the window. His friends raised their eyes, their smiles guarded.

The big kid led the others into the shop. Lillie grabbed her purse. Tension pounded across her forehead that felt as if it would explode. She stumbled out of the chair, relieved to find Dawson walking toward her.

"What's wrong?" he asked, as if sensing her distress.

She nodded toward the boys. The teenager with the baggy pants said something to the guy behind him as he sidled down the aisle. Nearing her table, the kid stopped short.

His eyes focused first on Dawson and then on the weapon visible on his hip. The teen pursed his lips and shrugged, then pointed the other two boys to a large table in the back of the shop, where three teenage girls waved. Dawson stared at them until they took their seats and huddled together, laughing.

Taking Lillie's arm, he ushered her toward the front of the shop and grabbed their coffees on the way outside.

She breathed in the cool winter air, feeling suddenly foolish. "I…I kept thinking someone was watching me."

"From all appearances, the three boys were meeting their girlfriends for coffee."

He was right, of course. "I'm a little paranoid."

"More than a little, but you have every right to be apprehensive, which confirms you should have stayed in Freemont."

She straightened her shoulders. "Then I would have been worried about you."

Dawson's lips twitched as he opened the car door for her. She slipped into the passenger seat and let out the breath she had been holding. His aftershave lingered in the car. Her insides turned to jelly, not because of the masculine scent, but because of everything that had happened.

Despite what she had told Dawson, she wanted to run

back to Freemont and the security of her home, but after the tragedy that had played out yesterday morning, her home was no longer a safe haven.

Dawson started the ignition and pulled into the stream of traffic. She stared at his strong hands gripping the wheel and knew her life had changed forever.

For better or for worse?

Definitely for the worse.

Dawson couldn't stop thinking about the prison interview. Leonard Simpson had confirmed Granger's story, but he had also mentioned the chaplain who preached words of love and forgiveness. Without prompting from Dawson, the convict had also shared Granger's belief that his prayers had led the University of Georgia law students to review his case and seek to right a wrong.

After a number of years on the job, most CID agents had a sixth sense about those who chose to walk on the path of darkness, and Dawson's gut feelings usually proved to be right. This time, he couldn't come to terms with his father's newfound faith, yet Leonard seemed convinced of Granger's transformation.

How could someone who turned his back on his own child find solace in the arms of a just God? As far as Dawson was concerned, Granger's change of heart was just a convict trying to come to grips with his past. Right now, Dawson needed to keep his eyes open and focused on the case.

He turned his attention back to Lillie. "Leonard Simpson verified everything Granger said on the video."

"Do you believe the story about the college kid and the murdered women?"

"Guys like to brag. Having a tale to tell, like the bar incident, gives a convict status. That's why we're going to visit his dad."

Dawson's phone rang. He raised the cell to his ear. "Timmons."

"My name's Jessica Baxter. You contacted the newspaper last night and said you wanted to talk about the MLK Missing Women."

Dawson flicked his gaze to Lillie. "The reporter," he mouthed before pushing the phone closer against his ear.

"I'm with the Criminal Investigation Division at Fort Rickman, Georgia," he told the woman. "We're investigating a homicide that occurred approximately twenty-five years ago in Freemont. I'm trying to determine if that murder is related to the three women who went missing in Atlanta."

"What do you want to know?" the journalist asked.

"How did you determine the disappearances of the women were related?"

"The girls lived in the Techwood Drive area of Atlanta."

"The projects near the Georgia Tech campus?"

"That's right. The area was torn down just before the 1996 Summer Olympics."

"Surely more than three women have disappeared in the city. Did you have other evidence to link them in addition to where they lived?"

"Printed T-shirts were left in their cars."

The journalist had Dawson's full attention. "Go on."

"The shirts were custom-made, similar to what college kids wear for special-event weekends. These particular shirts were to commemorate the MLK weekend."

"Did the police determine where they had been purchased?"

"Unfortunately, no. The cops came up empty-handed."

"And no additional women went missing?"

"That's right."

"What about your gut, Ms. Baxter?"

"How's that?" she asked.

"What's your gut tell you about the missing women?"

"They were murdered, and a serial killer was on the loose for those three years. I never could determine what stopped him from killing again."

She paused for a moment before adding, "I always thought the killer was trying to leave a message or a clue or a warning, perhaps."

"What kind of warning?"

"Who knows? I'm just telling you what I thought back then. The women disappeared more than twenty-five years ago. Their bodies have never been found, and the killer could be still on the loose. You might be the right man to bring him to justice."

"I'll let you know if I find him."

"I'll be praying for your safety and your success."

NINE

Dawson drove along the winding two-lane that wove through an older residential area in the suburbs of Atlanta. Lillie checked the street addresses, searching for the house where Leonard Simpson's parents lived. The community had been beautiful at one time, but the homes had aged, and many had fallen into disrepair.

On the way, they had passed a number of vacant strip malls and closed gas stations, providing further evidence of the neighborhood's decline with the passage of time.

Lillie pointed to a faded number painted on the curb. "Two-forty. The next house on this side of the street should be two-forty-two."

Dawson pulled into the driveway and helped Lillie from the car. His gaze focused on the one-story ranch with a small, screened side porch and two large oak trees that would provide shade in the summer.

Together they walked along a cracked sidewalk toward the small front porch. A handmade sign had been taped over the doorbell. *Bell Broken. Knock.*

Following the instructions, Dawson rapped twice. Footsteps sounded inside the house.

A lock turned, and the door opened a crack. Eyes stared at them over a chain lock still in place.

"Mrs. Simpson?" He held up his identification. "I'm Special Agent Dawson Timmons, from the Criminal Investigation Division at Fort Rickman."

The elderly woman read his ID then searched his face as if ensuring he matched his picture.

"Is this about Leonard?" she asked.

Dawson nodded. "We saw him earlier today and wanted to confirm information he provided."

The guardedness in her expression lifted. "You talked to my boy?"

"Yes, ma'am. He looked healthy, ma'am."

"And sends his love," Lillie added before she introduced herself.

"Just a minute." Mrs. Simpson closed the door. The guard chain rattled before she opened the door, this time wide. "Why don't you folks come in and tell me about Leonard."

"Thank you, ma'am." Dawson waited until Lillie stepped across the threshold before he followed her inside. The living room was neat and clean.

"Sit down, please." Mrs. Simpson pointed them towards the couch. "I could perk a pot of coffee."

Dawson held up his hand. "Thank you, ma'am, but that won't be necessary."

"Perhaps some sweet tea?" she offered.

"A glass of tea would be very nice," Lillie said before Dawson could decline the offer.

The old woman's face twisted into a smile. "I baked cookies this morning. They'll taste good with the cool drink."

"Harriet?" a male voice called from the rear of the house.

"Yes, dear." She hesitated, waiting for a reply. When none came, she glanced at her guests. "That's my husband, Charles. He stays in bed most days, but he loves when people visit."

She motioned them toward a narrow hallway. "Follow me. You can chat with him while I get the tea and cookies."

Dawson nodded optimistically at Lillie.

"Charles, these are some nice army folks who know Leonard," Mrs. Simpson said as they entered the bedroom.

The elderly man sat propped up against a pile of pillows with a heavy crocheted afghan thrown over the bedding, giving another layer of warmth to his fragile body.

His wife introduced them and then asked Dawson to open two folding aluminum chairs.

"It's good to meet you, sir." Dawson arranged a chair at the foot of the bed and invited Lillie to sit.

"These people talked to Leonard today, dear."

Recognition played over Charles's face.

Harriet excused herself and headed for the kitchen while Dawson settled into the second chair, which he positioned closer to the infirmed man's bedside.

"Your son looked fit, Mr. Simpson. He's doing well."

"Leonard…" The old man drew out the name. "He's a good boy."

His eyes glistened with pride for a son who had killed a convenience-store clerk in an armed-robbery attempt. Perhaps age or dementia had obscured Mr. Simpson's memory of his son's felony offense.

"Sir, I'm with law enforcement at Fort Rickman, two hours south of Atlanta. I'm investigating a murder that occurred in nearby Freemont, Georgia, which may have ties to a young man you spoke with at your bar years ago. Leonard said one of your customers talked about three possible homicides. Do you remember that conversation, sir?"

The old man closed his eyes. Dawson feared he had drifted to sleep.

"Do you recall a customer who talked about burying women in steel drums?" Lillie asked from the foot of the bed.

The tired eyes blinked open. He lifted his shoulders ever so slightly off the pillow, attempting to see her more clearly.

She stood, walked to the opposite side of his bed and patted his hand. "I'm sure your customers sometimes told you more than you wanted to hear?"

He nodded, his gnarled fingers picking at the afghan.

"The young man's story about killing women troubled Charles," his wife said as she stepped back into the room, no doubt having overheard the conversation from the hallway. She carried a tray with four glasses of tea and a plate of sugar cookies.

Placing the tray on a small table in the corner of the room, she handed Lillie and Dawson their drinks and offered them cookies, which they both accepted.

"Thank you, ma'am." Dawson bit into the rich shortbread. "Delicious."

Harriet beamed as she stuck a straw in Charles's glass and held it to his lips. The old man drank greedily and nodded with appreciation when she returned the half-empty glass to the bed stand.

"I told Charles he couldn't take everything to heart, but the story affected me as well." Harriet patted her chest. "The boy said his brother had killed three women. Charles notified the police, hoping they could track down the boy and the victims."

"The Atlanta police?" Dawson asked.

The older woman nodded. "They said a lot of kids tell stories when they're under the influence, but Charles felt there was some truth to this young man's tale."

Dawson leaned closer to the bed. "Do you remember what he looked like, sir?"

The older man rubbed his chin and stared into space.

Harriet helped him out. "Remember, dear, you said he reminded you of our boy."

"Brown hair, brown eyes, medium build?" Dawson ticked off the convict's description and stared down at the old man.

When Charles failed to respond, Harriet nudged his arm. "You remember, don't you, dear?"

"College boy," he said at last.

"How do you know he was in college?" Dawson asked. "Did he mention the name of his school?"

Mr. Simpson pointed a shaky hand to his own chest. "His shirt."

"Did it say something about the MLK holiday?"

"G—"

"UGA?" The University of Georgia campus was in Athens, about an hour drive from Atlanta.

Charles closed his eyes for a long moment. "G…T."

"Georgia Tech? Did you ever see the guy again?"

The old man shook his head.

"What did he tell you, sir?" Dawson needed to ensure Leonard's details were accurate.

"His…his brother killed three women. Buried them in steel drums."

"Do you remember the year?"

A frown played across Charles's drawn face.

Harriet helped him out. "Leonard went to jail that spring, Charles. It's been twenty-five years."

She turned to look at Dawson with serious eyes. "I've been praying for our son ever since, and for those women as well." Wringing her hands, she added, "I've been praying for the killer too. That he'll tell the police where he buried the bodies. Think what those families have endured by not being able to come to closure about their children's disappearances."

Dawson continued to question Charles, but neither he

nor Harriet could recall anything else about the young man that night.

After thanking the couple for their hospitality and help, Dawson and Lillie headed back to his car. Before he backed out of the drive, the Simpsons' door flew open. Harriet flagged them down from the porch.

Lowering his window, Dawson called to her. "Is something wrong, ma'am?"

"It's Charles. He remembered the boy in the bar."

A plane flew overhead, and the sound drowned out her voice. "What's that, ma'am?"

She cupped her hands around her mouth. "The boy from Georgia Tech..."

Dawson waited until a car drove past the house.

"Could you repeat what you just said?"

She walked down the steps and stood on the sidewalk. "Charles remembered something else about the boy from Georgia Tech." She pointed to her head. "The boy had red hair."

"Is Billy Everett the redhead?" Lillie asked as Dawson pulled out of the driveway.

"From what Pritchard mentioned, it seems unlikely he went to Georgia Tech."

"But the college kid said his brother committed the crimes."

"Then we need to find out if Billy Everett has a brother with red hair who attended school in Atlanta."

Lillie stared out the window as they left the Simpsons' neighborhood, lost in her own thoughts. Dawson seemed focused on the road, and they rode in silence for a period of time, until the freeway appeared in the distance.

He glanced at his watch. "It's late in the day, and we

haven't eaten. Let's get some food before we head back to Freemont."

"There's a diner about thirty miles south of the city that's known for fast service and home cooking," she suggested.

"Sounds good."

Snippets of information kept floating through Lillie's mind. "Maybe if we go over what we know so far, something might fall into place."

Dawson smiled. "You're thinking like a cop. Go ahead."

She held up her finger. "First of all, we're looking for a Georgia Tech college student with red hair?"

Dawson nodded. "That's right, and if what he said in the bar was true, his brother killed three women. Any idea how many kids from Freemont High get accepted to Tech each year?"

She shrugged. "Not many. The school has stiff entrance requirements. Standardized test scores have to be high, and good grades are a must."

"I'll call the high school on Monday and see if the guidance counselor can give me a list of anyone who attended Tech twenty-five to thirty years ago. Hopefully, the records will still be on file."

"Excuse my pessimism, but it's not much to go on, Dawson."

"Sometimes the smallest scrap of information can be the missing link that pulls an entire case together."

"What if the Georgia Tech student and his brother weren't from Freemont?" Lillie asked. "Suppose they were from Atlanta or knew my mother when she lived in the city."

Dawson nodded. "The killer could have found out where she was living and come after her in Freemont."

Instead of finding clarity, Lillie was more confused than

ever. "If he killed my mother in Freemont, why had he killed the women in Atlanta first?"

"When were you born?" he asked.

"October twentieth." She provided the year.

"The first woman listed on the flash drive disappeared three months after your birth."

"What does that prove?"

Dawson shook his head and let out a deep breath. "Nothing. But let's go the other direction."

"You mean nine months before I was born?"

He nodded. "That's right. Nine months earlier would be the month in which you were conceived."

Lillie did the math. "That would have been January."

"As in the MLK weekend." Dawson's face was serious as he turned to her. "I think we may have uncovered a connection."

"I'm not following you?"

"Your mother's pregnancy may have upset the killer." Dawson shrugged. "I'm not sure of the reason, but he could have been angry or jealous so he strikes out at other women for three years, always over the MLK weekend."

"To get back at my mother?"

"Maybe. His rage could also have been directed toward your father."

"So he kills three women, then finally comes after my mother." Lillie let out a deep breath. "Which means she died because of me."

Dawson shook his head. "You didn't do anything wrong. He was upset about your mother's pregnancy, not at you."

The diner came into view. "Let's get something to eat. We can pick up where we left off after dinner."

Although Lillie was hungry, she didn't know if food would help unravel the threads of the past that were tied together in a huge knot. Would she ever know what happened so long ago?

She glanced at Dawson as he pulled into the restaurant parking lot. Before Granger died, he had asked her to free them from the past. Would the truth set them free or handicap them even more?

TEN

Full from dinner, Lillie felt her eyes grow heavy on the drive back to Freemont. Dawson had ordered the meat loaf with fresh green beans and mashed potatoes, and she had followed suit. The meal was delicious. Then he had ordered apple pie à la mode and insisted she indulge as well.

At the cozy roadside restaurant, they'd talked about everything except the investigation. His hand had touched hers twice when they reached for the saltshaker at the same time.

Lillie had to admit she enjoyed being with Dawson. He was committed to his job, and like the other army guys she knew, he loved his country and felt privileged to be able to serve. He also liked small towns and Southern cooking and sweet tea, which he had gulped down along with two refills.

The waitress had told them to come back soon, and Dawson said they would. Not that his comment meant anything, but the thought of returning to the city with him, perhaps to tour the aquarium—which they both wanted to see—and stopping again at the quaint restaurant on the way home made her smile.

"What's so funny?" he said, pulling his eyes from the road.

The sun had set, and his face was shadowed by the lights

from the dash, causing more than a tingle of interest to meander lazily along her skin.

She shook her head. "Just thinking about the nice dinner. Thank you."

"Thank you for suggesting the restaurant. We'll have to do it again."

Another wave of energy, only this time it did more than meander. She sat up in the seat, knowing her thoughts were getting way ahead of where their relationship was going.

Note to self. Dawson is investigating his father's death, not taking me home from a date.

For some reason, she preferred thinking about the date and found her eyes growing heavy once again.

"I'm not good company." She laughed.

"You don't have to worry, Lillie. Go ahead and close your eyes."

He was right. She didn't have to worry with Dawson. For so long, she'd been on her own. The McKinneys had been there for her growing up, but her foster parents had tried to keep her insulated from the town gossips with homeschooling and living on the farm. Lillie had never felt a part of anything, not even the country church community that had welcomed her with open arms.

The problem wasn't with the congregation or the McKinneys. It was with her. She always kept up her guard so she wouldn't be hurt again. She'd even kept up her guard with God.

Tonight she didn't want to think about anything that had to do with the past. She wanted to think about eating mashed potatoes and gravy and meat loaf with a man whose eyes made her think of bright sunshine and blue skies.

Lillie's cheeks burned when she realized she had drifted to sleep and had been dreaming about Dawson.

He took her hand in his own and rubbed his fingers over

hers, which made her flesh feel alive and brought delightful tingles to her neck.

Their exit appeared in the distance. Dawson squeezed her fingers before he released her hand to make the turn. Once off the exit ramp, he steered the car along the back road that led past the Hi-Way Motel.

They were back to where they had been yesterday morning. He was the cop, and Lillie was a witness in the investigation.

What had she been thinking? As soon as the investigation was over, Dawson would be working on something else, and maybe in the future he'd be reassigned to another military post far away from Fort Rickman and Freemont.

She pulled her hand through her hair, chastising herself for being so foolish. She wasn't made to share life with a man. Especially a good man like Dawson.

She had her job, her house and a future working at Fort Rickman. She didn't need anything else. But when she looked at Dawson again, she realized she was deluding herself. A happily ever after was what every girl dreamed of having in her life. Although not every dream came true.

Surely, Lillie was asking too much.

Dawson had a hard time keeping his eyes on the road with Lillie sitting next to him. He flicked his gaze toward her when she wasn't looking and studied the fullness of her lips. It made him want to pull to the side of the road and take her in his arms. Which, of course, he didn't do, nor would he while the investigation was still in progress.

Besides, Lillie wasn't interested in him except for the help he could provide in finding out about her mother's death, which she had mentioned more than once. Although during dinner she had seemed to relax and enjoy herself. When she laughed, his own mood lightened as if they were connected and nothing could pull them apart. Foolish of him to think that way.

She had drifted off to sleep, and he hadn't been able to stop himself from reaching for her hand. At the time, it seemed such a natural response after their day together.

Passing the Hi-Way Motel brought back memories of yesterday morning. Granger had hidden Billy Everett's picture in a spot where Dawson had failed to look. Now it appeared the redhead might be involved.

The train trestle appeared overhead. Dawson squinted into the darkness, trying to see what was hanging from the bridge.

He lifted his foot off the accelerator. Blood rushed to his neck. Adrenaline, mixed with a chilling fear, turned his veins to ice.

A boulder, large, gray, deadly, dropped from overhead.

He swerved. The huge rock crashed against the edge of his right fender with a loud *whack*.

Feeling the car lurch, Lillie gasped. Her hand reached protectively for the dashboard.

Dawson pulled to the curb. Throwing open the door, he stepped into the night, his eyes searching the bridge for any sign of the person or persons who had hurled the giant boulder.

Seeing nothing except the pine trees that bordered the road, he rounded the car and studied the deep dent in his front fender.

Lillie watched him through the window, her eyes wide. Dawson's stomach sickened, realizing if he hadn't swerved, the rock would have shattered the windshield and crashed into Lillie.

He turned away, unable to look at her, because all he could see was her bloodied body and the terrible what-could-have-been consequences of the falling rock.

The car door opened. She stepped onto the pavement and stared up at the now-empty trestle. "It wasn't an accident, was it?"

He swallowed down the bile that had filled his throat. "Rocks don't drop from the sky or from train trestles."

Pulling his phone from his pocket, Dawson tapped in a series of digits. "I'm calling Pritchard. The entire area needs to be searched."

To his credit, the police officer promised to be there within a few minutes. Dawson didn't want Lillie to wait in the open for the cruiser, not when she was a target. He slipped his arm over her shoulders, as if his closeness would offer protection.

"You need to get in the car," he said. "Hunker down in the seat. I'll stay out here until Pritchard arrives."

"You're worried someone's still in the area?"

"He's probably long gone by now." Dawson smiled, trying to make light of the situation yet knowing full well that Lillie saw beyond his attempt to soft-pedal the deadly seriousness of what had happened. "I just want to keep you safe."

He squeezed her shoulder and opened the door. She hesitated before slipping onto the leather seat, then hit the lock and smiled weakly when he gave her a thumbs-up through the window.

With determined steps, Dawson walked to the rear of his Camry and felt under the fender. A siren sounded, approaching from town. He brushed off his hands as the police sedan pulled to the side of the road. Pritchard stepped onto the pavement.

A second car braked to a stop. Pritchard instructed the two officers who emerged from the cruiser to climb the rise and look for anything that might indicate a person had been on the trestle.

Once they hustled off, the lead cop approached Dawson.

Still sitting in the front seat, Lillie glanced at Pritchard over her shoulder.

"Evening, ma'am," he said through the window.

Turning back to Dawson, he raised his brow. "You folks out for a nighttime drive?"

"We were coming back from Atlanta."

"Something happening in the city I should know about?"

Dawson didn't want to divulge anything. At least not yet. If and when he pulled the pieces of this very strange case together in some type of order, maybe then he'd be more forthcoming.

"We went out for dinner."

"Long way for a meal." Pritchard stared at Dawson with dark eyes. "Ms. Beaumont is a witness in a murder investigation. Seems strange you'd ask her out on a date."

"It wasn't a date."

Lillie stepped from the car and joined the men.

"How was Atlanta, ma'am?"

Dawson kept his gaze fixed on the trestle. Pritchard was fishing, trying to get Lillie to divulge the real reason they had been in the city.

She wrapped her arms around her waist. "Getting away from Freemont for the day was good for both of us."

"Sir," one of the officers called down to Pritchard. "We found a gum wrapper."

"Bag it." Pritchard glanced at Dawson. "Although a gum wrapper doesn't prove anyone was lying in wait."

Dawson tensed. "The boulder couldn't have dropped on its own."

Frustrated with the small-town cop who seemed to have his own agenda, Dawson stooped down and felt under the fender of his car.

"Looking for something?" Pritchard asked.

"A hunch. That's all." Dawson's fingers touched something small and metallic. He yanked the attachment free and stood to examine the device in the light from the police cruiser.

"What is it?" Lillie asked.

Dawson turned it over in his hand. "A magnetic GPS tracking device."

She raised her brow. "They followed us from Atlanta."

Pritchard stepped closer. "Someone thought you were doing more than enjoying a good meal."

Dawson didn't respond to the cop. He was looking at Lillie. No wonder the killer had been able to pinpoint their whereabouts and the exact moment when they drove under the trestle.

The rock had missed the windshield, but only barely. Dawson had to make sure from now on nothing hurt Lillie. Not an out-of-control SUV or a hurled boulder or a killer who seemed to have her in his sights.

Lillie waited in the Camry while Pritchard and the two other officers returned to their squad cars. Worry strained Dawson's face when he slid into the seat next to her.

He gave her a tepid smile that did nothing to lift her spirits. No matter where they turned, the killer—or killers—seemed one step ahead of them.

"I gave Pritchard the tracking device." Dawson started the engine and pulled onto the roadway. "He'll try to determine who purchased it and where."

"I don't see how they'll be able to find the buyer. In fact, I doubt we'll ever know who's behind all this."

Dawson held out his hand. She placed hers in his, buoyed by the warmth of his touch.

"Finding the GPS system was a plus for our side. No doubt they hoped to keep track of our movements for days."

"How long has it been attached to your car?"

"Probably not more than a few hours. We were inside the prison for quite a while. The parking lot was accessible to anyone who happened by." He squeezed her hand. "The important thing is that you're safe."

"And tired. I'll be glad to get home."

"With everything that's happened, I don't want you to stay in your house tonight. You can get a room on post in the Lodge."

She sighed. "I know you're thinking of my own well-being, but I want to go home."

"You want everything to go back to how it was just a few days ago."

Dawson was right. That was exactly what she wanted.

"What about your foster parents?" he asked. "You said they live in the country. The killer or killers might not look for you there."

"Or they might and then my foster parents would be placed in danger. Besides, I don't want them to know what happened. They rarely leave their farm, so I'm sure they haven't heard about Granger's death yet."

"Hasn't the story run in the local papers?"

"The Sunday edition went to press a few days ago. The next issue won't be out until Wednesday."

"Your parents deserve to know what happened, Lillie. Call them and ask if you can stay until Monday morning. By then, this might be behind us."

"I think you're being overly optimistic."

"Please, Lillie, if you won't do it for yourself, then do it for me. I don't want anything to happen to you."

Dawson's concern touched her deeply, and an unexpected lump formed in her throat. He sounded sincere, but she was a witness in his father's murder investigation, which was probably the reason he was worried about her safety.

No matter what he had meant by the comment, she knew

complying with his request was the wisest and safest thing to do.

"Drive me home, Dawson. I need to pack a few items, no matter where I stay tonight."

He smiled. "Now you're being smart."

Lillie didn't feel smart. She felt trapped in the middle of a huge maze. Glancing at Dawson, she wondered if he felt the same way.

Once his father's murder was solved, he would move on to the next case. Where would that leave Lillie? At home in her little house with only the memory of the CID agent who had made her feel safe.

ELEVEN

Dawson was relieved when Lillie agreed to spend the rest of the weekend with her foster family, although she insisted he also spend the night there.

"They have a guest room," she told him. "And my mother's a great cook."

The thought of another home-cooked meal was tempting. An even stronger draw was getting to know the folks who had taken Lillie in as a child. They had to be good people.

The cop side of him hoped they might provide additional information about her mother's death and Granger's trial. He also hoped Lillie would let down her guard and share some of her own struggle with him.

Dawson pulled into the driveway of her own small, secluded home. The crime-scene tape had been removed from the front porch, but they still entered her house through the kitchen, as if the spot where Granger had died was consecrated ground upon which neither of them wanted to tread.

Once inside, Lillie headed to her room, while Dawson lounged on the couch. He closed his eyes and felt the tension that had built up over the past two days ease.

A nice place to call home. Surprised by the thought that came unbidden, he stood, realizing he had become much too comfortable. Lillie appeared soon thereafter with an overnight bag in hand, which he took from her and carried to his car.

Driving through Freemont, Dawson kept watch in his rearview mirror to ensure they weren't being followed. As an added precaution, he made a series of turns and checked for any sign of a white SUV. Once he was certain they were on their own, he followed Lillie's promptings and eventually headed west into the rural farmland.

Lillie directed him along a number of back roads. Hopefully, the rather difficult-to-find location of the McKinney farm would keep trouble at bay, or at least prevent anyone who wasn't familiar with the area from finding her.

"My mother will like you," Lillie said when Freemont was far behind them.

"What about your dad?"

"He'll want to know what you do and why you're with his daughter. Mom will be more direct. She'll think we're dating. If the conversation turns to weddings, just play dumb."

He laughed. "She thinks it's time for her daughter to find a husband?"

Lillie smiled. "In her day, women married young. She's afraid I'll be a spinster for life."

Dawson turned his gaze to Lillie's long legs and slender body and tried not to chuckle at her foster mother's concern for her daughter's future. The only reason Lillie wasn't taken was because she hadn't found the right guy.

At least, he hoped she didn't have someone waiting in the wings. Or stationed at another army post.

Shoving the thought aside, he said, "So what happens if they ask about my intentions for their daughter?"

Lillie glanced at him, her lips smiling and her cheeks pink with embarrassment. "If they go that far, I'll step in and rescue you. They mean well, but they can both be overly exuberant."

"You're lucky, Lillie."

She raised her brow and stared back at him. "You mean because they took me in?"

"Because they love you."

She bit her lip. "Sometimes I think I didn't appreciate them enough growing up." She was quiet for a long moment and then asked, "How's your relationship with your mom?"

He weighed his answer. "It's hard to explain. She always tried to justify the mistakes she made in life."

Lillie shifted in her seat. He could feel her gaze. "You weren't a mistake, Dawson."

"My mother claimed falling in love with Granger was the problem. She expended too much effort trying to convince herself she didn't love him and that he wasn't worthy of her love."

"How did that affect you?"

"If my father wasn't worthy, I figured I wasn't either. I kept hoping my dad would come back to Cotton Grove and take me away with him."

Lillie arched a brow. "Did he ever return?"

"Only once. One of my friends saw him with my mom. I was in school at the time. I thought he'd pull me out of class, but he didn't."

"From what Leonard Simpson said, your mom didn't want Granger in your life."

Dawson swallowed, hoping to end a conversation that was headed where he didn't want to go.

"Did you ever ask her about your dad?" Lillie pressed.

"I learned early on not to bring up his name."

"Where's your mom now?"

"Still in Cotton Grove. She works for a local grocery chain."

"But you don't talk to her?"

He shrugged. "I call her at Christmas and holidays."

Dawson kept his gaze on the road, and they rode in silence until Lillie indicated the next turn and then pointed to a small farmhouse that sat on a rise in the distance. Floodlights illuminated the two-story white structure and a portion of the long driveway and expansive front yard.

Two wooden rockers sat on the porch.

Dawson parked next to the house and helped Lillie from the car, wondering how the welcome home would play out. "Maybe you should have called your parents."

"I did when I was packing," Lillie said. "They're expecting us."

Dawson should have felt relieved. He grabbed Lillie's overnight bag and headed for the front door, concerned he had made a mistake by agreeing to stay the night.

The door opened before they climbed onto the porch and a short woman with a round face, welcoming grin and arms held wide stepped from the house. "Hello, darlin'. Daddy and I were just saying we thought you should be arriving any minute."

After Lillie hugged her mother, she moved aside and motioned Dawson forward. Without waiting for an introduction, Mrs. McKinney wrapped him in a bear hug that made him smile.

A man, probably in his early seventies, with gray hair and a sun-dried face, came onto the porch. His arms were extended equally as wide as his wife's had been.

"How's my little girl?" he said, embracing Lillie. "Now that you've got that good job on post, we don't see you enough, honey."

Lillie kissed his cheek. "You and Mother can always come to visit me in Freemont."

"You know we're homebodies." Her father stretched out his hand. "Who's this young man?"

Lillie smiled at Dawson, who returned the older man's

handshake. "Dawson Timmons, sir. It's a pleasure to meet you."

"Thanks for bringing Lillie home to us. Come in out of the cold." Her father took Lillie's bag and motioned both of them inside.

Mrs. McKinney patted Dawson's arm. "Lillie said you had dinner in Atlanta, but I hope you saved room for dessert. I baked a chocolate cake earlier today."

He looked at Lillie for help.

"Dawson would love some cake, Mother." Lillie winked at him.

"How about you, dear? Surely you can eat a little piece. There's ice cream too."

"Just some cake, Mother. Half a slice."

"Where's your bag?" her father asked Dawson before he closed the door.

"In the car, sir. I'll get it later."

The house was comfortable and inviting, and Dawson instantly felt at ease with the McKinneys' warm welcome. The women headed for the kitchen while Dawson stopped in the living room to admire the assortment of firearms displayed in an antique gun rack.

Hanging on the wall next to the weapons were framed awards, evidence that Lillie's father was an accomplished marksman.

"That's quite a collection of guns and awards, sir."

"My daddy always said a man needs to be able to protect his land and his family."

"Yes, sir."

"Who wants coffee?" Mrs. McKinney called from the kitchen.

"Be right there, Sarah." Mr. McKinney pursed his lips as he turned his full attention to Dawson. "You're not a stranger to guns."

"No, sir."

"What are you packing tonight?"

"A Glock, sir. I'm with the Criminal Investigation Division stationed at Fort Rickman."

The older man nodded. "The Glock's a good weapon."

"Yes, sir." Dawson pulled in a breath. "There's something I'd like to discuss with you, sir. Mrs. McKinney needs to know as well."

"Let's have some cake. Then we can talk." Without commenting further, Mr. McKinney headed for the kitchen.

Standing at the counter, Mrs. McKinney cut the cake and arranged the slices on four plates. "There's a potluck lunch after church tomorrow. Everyone will enjoy meeting Dawson."

The smell of fresh-perked coffee filled the kitchen.

Dawson tried to catch Lillie's gaze. "I doubt I'll be able to stay for church, ma'am."

"Do you attend services in the city?"

"The city?" he asked.

"Freemont." Lillie helped him out.

After taking the cake plates from her mother, Lillie placed them on the table. "Dawson lives at Fort Rickman, Mother. I'm sure he goes to church there."

"How nice." Mrs. McKinney smiled broadly.

He didn't have the heart to tell the charming woman that his relationship with God was presently on hold.

"We'd love having you join us tomorrow, if you can spare the time."

Dawson was outnumbered. He could confront armed criminals without flinching, but he had trouble worming his way out of attending church with the McKinneys.

As he bit into the cake and allowed the rich chocolate to melt in his mouth, he smiled at the warm family dynamic. Mrs. McKinney and her husband were committed to one another, and Lillie, whether she realized it or not, was the center of their world.

Bringing up a topic such as her biological mother's murder seemed out of place at this moment. Lillie was right. He needed to bide his time.

After the dishes were washed and put away, Dawson knew he needed to broach the subject Lillie continued to ignore. He glanced at her over the top of his coffee cup.

She shrugged and then sighed. "Mother and Dad, there was an incident outside my house yesterday morning. A…a man was shot."

"Oh, good Lord in heaven." Mrs. McKinney patted her chest. Eyes wide, she plopped down onto one of the kitchen chairs and stared at Lillie. "Who was it, dear?"

"Granger Ford, Mama."

Her father threw an angry glance at Dawson. "Isn't he still in prison?"

Dawson cleared his throat. "The court reviewed his case, sir. DNA testing overturned the validity of the previous evidence. He was released from prison two weeks ago."

"Who killed him?" Mr. McKinney's gaze remained fixed on Dawson.

"We're trying to track down those who were involved, sir."

Dawson and Lillie quickly gave her parents an overview of what had happened. Neither of them mentioned the driver of the SUV who had run Lillie off the road. Nor did they discuss their day trip to Atlanta or that Granger Ford was Dawson's father. Some things were better left unsaid.

"I felt Lillie shouldn't stay alone in her house and suggested she come here for the weekend," Dawson finally concluded.

Mrs. McKinney reached for Lillie's hand. "I never liked you living by yourself."

"Mama, it's just for the weekend. Dawson feels a suspect may be in custody by Monday."

Her father didn't look optimistic, and her mother shook her head and tsked.

Dawson turned to Mr. McKinney. "The thing is, sir, I knew you would be able to keep Lillie safe. I feel even more confident after seeing your marksmanship awards and gun collection."

Her father nodded, as if somewhat placated by Dawson's acknowledgment of his ability. "If Granger didn't kill Irene Beaumont, then who did?"

"I don't know, sir. That's what the Freemont police are trying to uncover."

"But you're working on the case?" her father asked.

"I've been assigned to protect your daughter. I was hoping you and I could work together over the weekend."

Later when the McKinneys had gone to bed and Lillie was in her room, Dawson went outside to get the gym bag he carried in the car.

He glanced around the expansive front yard and surrounding fields and was stirred by a desire to work the earth. Mr. McKinney had turned off the floodlights, and the sky seemed alive with the glittering stars.

The door to the house opened, and Lillie stepped onto the porch. She waited until he had his bag in hand and then met him on the stairs.

"I told you my mother would want to feed you."

"They're good people, Lillie." He placed his gear on the top step.

She nodded. "I know they are. They gave me a life, and I'll always be grateful."

"But?" He heard the hesitation in her voice.

"I always worry they'll be taken away from me. Just as my mother was."

"Which is why you didn't want to come here."

"And why I didn't want them to know what had happened. I keep thinking if I don't talk about something, it might not be true." She tapped her foot against the bottom porch railing. "As I mentioned, growing up I thought my mother had abandoned me. That's tough on a kid. Then when her body was found—"

She looked into the night and shrugged. "Somehow I couldn't get past all those years of thinking she had left me. I closed her out of my life, and I never let her back in."

He reached for her hand and ran his fingers through hers. "You've got to forgive yourself. You were young and had gone through a terrible experience."

"I thought if I had been a better daughter or if I hadn't been afraid of storms, my mother would have loved me. Every time another storm hit, I was overcome with fright and thought my actions continued to keep her away. Before long, I convinced myself that I didn't want her back in my life."

He glanced up at the house. "Did you tell them how you felt?"

She shook her head. "I kept everything boxed up inside me. They had done so much. I couldn't let them know how I really felt."

"You could talk to them now."

She shook her head. "It's my problem. I'll deal with it."

"You don't have to always be so strong." He stepped closer to her and touched her hair, which was what he had wanted to do since yesterday morning.

Her eyes searched his, and her lips opened ever so slightly. The earth stood still for one long moment. He drank in her beauty and longed to pull her into his arms.

Almost without thinking, he reached for her. She shifted closer, and then, as if both of them had been waiting for this moment, he lowered his lips to hers.

Her mouth was soft and warm and welcoming, and every fiber of his being wanted to keep kissing her forever. Although his eyes were closed, he was sure fireworks illuminated the night sky. He could almost see bursts of color as his heart exploded in his chest. All he could think of was holding her tight for the rest of his life.

She pulled back too quickly. He wanted to kiss her again, but seeing her brow crease and the downturn of her mouth, he dropped his hands to his sides. Instantly, he felt a sense of detachment and a stab of confusion as she stepped back and wrapped her hands around her arms.

"I need to go back inside."

He nodded. She was probably upset that he had kissed her. Without further explanation, she climbed the steps and entered the house.

Dawson didn't follow her. He couldn't. He needed time in the cold night air to steady his pounding heart. His leg throbbed, which he hadn't noticed when Lillie was in his arms.

A car drove along the road. Dawson watched it slowly disappear into the distance. Lillie would be safe here, especially with Mr. McKinney's desire to protect his family.

What he had always wanted most in life was a loving home where he could be accepted. Tonight he'd had a taste of how good that life could be, but this was Lillie's home, not his.

When he stepped back into the house, he found her father waiting for him. "Lillie went to bed."

Dawson knew there was more the man wanted to say. "Yes, sir."

Mr. McKinney pointed to the kitchen. "I put on a pot of decaf. We need to talk."

Dawson followed Mr. McKinney into the kitchen. He was back to being the special agent. Lillie was a witness to a murder who needed to be protected, even though he wanted her to be so much more in his life. Right now, the investigation took precedence, and Lillie's safety was his paramount concern. Her father probably felt the same way.

But what about Dawson?

Whenever he was with Lillie, he knew he had to guard his heart. She could be his downfall.

Lillie got up early and followed the smell of eggs and bacon to the kitchen. Her father sat at the table, reading the Sunday paper and sipping from a steaming mug of coffee.

Her mother stood at the stove. "Can I fix you breakfast, darlin'?"

Lillie headed for the coffeepot. "Maybe when Dawson gets up."

"He's been outside for a couple hours." Her father's voice came from behind his paper. "Said he wanted to see the place. I took him down to the barn and the livestock pen. Filled him in on how a farm this size operates."

Lillie walked to the window and stared into the backyard, where Dawson was spreading hay for the livestock. "You put him to work?"

"Men like to stay busy, Lillie. Being outside in the fresh air is good for him. Besides, he wanted to help."

"He certainly is a nice young man," her mother said. The upturn in her tone told Lillie about the plans the older woman was already making.

"We're friends, Mother, which I told you over the phone when I called last night."

"Of course, dear. Your father and I are best friends."

Lillie smiled, knowing some battles couldn't be won.

Glancing out the window again, she watched Dawson add feed to the troughs. Then he stamped his feet on the frosty earth and brushed off his hands. "Looks like he's coming inside for breakfast."

"Grab a mug from the cupboard, Lillie, and pour him a fresh cup of coffee."

The back door opened, blowing in a gust of cold morning air as Dawson stepped inside, rosy cheeked and eyes twinkling as he looked at her. "Morning, sleepyhead."

His lazy voice and ruddy complexion, made even more pronounced by the brisk winter air, stirred something deep inside her. *Watch yourself,* a voice warned as a delicious tingle rolled over her body.

"Ready for some coffee?" she asked, trying to come back down to earth.

He held up his hands. "Let me wash up first."

Placing the filled mug on the table, Lillie took the plate her mother had fixed for Dawson and set it next to the coffee, along with silverware and a cloth napkin.

"How about you, dear?" her mother asked.

"I'll just have some fruit." Lillie reached for a banana and pear and placed them on a small plate.

Before she could get back to the table, Dawson had returned to the kitchen, filling the air with the clean scent of soap and the outdoors.

A girl could get used to that combination, she thought as she dropped into the chair he held.

His good manners weren't lost on her father, who always held the door for her mother. He stared at Dawson over the top of the paper and pursed his lips in approval before Dawson found his seat.

Lillie bowed her head as she silently gave thanks, noting Dawson followed her lead and hesitated before he picked up his fork.

"Delicious, Mrs. McKinney," he said after swallowing a rather hefty portion of eggs and grits.

"You worked up an appetite helping Walter."

"I enjoy working with my hands."

Once again, her father eyed Lillie over the paper. "There's an article in the Community Doings section about that new museum at Fort Rickman. The article said Karl Nelson's company won the bid."

"Nelson Construction has done a lot for the people in this town," her mother added as she joined them at the table with her own plate. "Although he's nothing like his father. Burl was a kind and patient man."

Her father folded the paper and raised his brow. "Burl had to have patience to stay with that wife of his."

Mrs. McKinney jabbed her husband's arm. "Now, Walter, no reason to repeat stories. At least Karl takes after his daddy."

"The community is invited to the opening ceremony," Lillie said. "I could get you special seats. You'd enjoy the speeches. The Fort Rickman Army Band will play."

"Why, dear, it sounds lovely, but your father and I rarely get to town. You spend the day with Dawson."

"I'll be working the event," he said.

Mrs. McKinney's eyes widened. "You're not expecting anything dangerous to happen, are you, Dawson?"

"No, ma'am. Just normal security issues." He glanced at Lillie for encouragement.

She smiled, feeling her cheeks warm and knowing the direction of the conversation needed to change. "Dawson's from Cotton Grove, Mama."

"A Georgia boy." Mrs. McKinney couldn't hide the pleasure in her voice. "How nice. Won't you have some banana bread?"

"Thank you, ma'am." Dawson took two large slices before asking, "You folks ever know a local guy named Billy

Everett? He attended Freemont High. Red hair. He's got a scar on his cheek."

Mrs. McKinney placed her fork on her plate. "Of course I remember Billy. His family was poor. He was the baby."

"Not the brightest kid around," her father added.

"Billy dropped out of school," Mrs. McKinney continued. "I heard he got into trouble with drugs and did some time in prison." Mrs. McKinney shook her head. "Such a shame."

"Prison does terrible things to a man." Mr. McKinney reached for his coffee and took a long swig of the hot brew. "I don't believe in rehabilitation. Doing time just makes a bad man even worse."

Lillie had never heard her father be so vindictive. "Some folks find God in prison," she said, hoping to turn the conversation in a more positive direction.

"I'm just glad we never had anyone in our family who ended up behind bars. It'd be a black mark for sure."

He folded the paper. "Now if you'll excuse me, I need to get ready for church."

Lillie looked at Dawson and the set of his jaw as he dropped the remainder of the banana bread onto his plate and pushed away from the table.

"Breakfast was delicious, Mrs. McKinney. I need to get back to Fort Rickman."

"Won't you join us for church?"

"Not today, ma'am."

"I'll get my things," Lillie said.

He looked at her, his gaze steady. "You stay here. I'll pick you up tomorrow morning."

"Dinner's at six," Mrs. McKinney said.

"Ma'am, you don't need me underfoot."

"Nonsense. I'm frying chicken. Easy enough to put another plate on the table. We'll expect you at six o'clock."

"Thank you, ma'am."

Lillie followed him to the door, wishing she could say something to soothe the rough moment that had to have hurt Dawson. "My father wasn't thinking."

"He said what he believes, Lillie. And he's right. Most cons return to a life of crime shortly after getting out of prison."

"Your dad was exonerated of any wrongdoing, Dawson."

"He was in prison for fifteen years. Things happen to a man behind bars."

Lillie reached for his hand. "On the phone, Granger told me he had made his peace with the Lord."

"Yeah? Too bad he never made peace with his son."

"He tried, Dawson."

"Maybe, but by then it was too late."

TWELVE

When Dawson arrived back at his BOQ, he was still stewing about Mr. McKinney's comment concerning ex-cons. Lillie's dad had no idea Dawson's father had been incarcerated, and although his comment troubled Dawson, her father had the right to his own opinion on such matters. Besides, Dawson knew the statistics fell in line with what the older man had mentioned.

Law-enforcement personnel were well aware that more than four in ten offenders returned to prison within three years of being released. Recidivism was a national problem and one with no easy solution.

The previous night, after Lillie had gone to bed, Mr. McKinney had talked openly about Irene Beaumont's death and his concern for his daughter. The McKinneys had taken her in as a terrorized four-year-old. When her mother's body had been unearthed, the middle-school-aged Lillie had suffered a setback, and both parents worried about her emotional health.

The prosecutor had talked to Lillie's foster father about Granger's trial. Mr. McKinney had been forthcoming with Dawson concerning his own fear that Granger's guilt had been too quickly decided.

At the time, the McKinneys had been focused on Lillie.

They wanted to ensure their daughter didn't experience another setback or more pain than what she had already suffered. In an effort to insulate her from the wagging tongues
in town, Mrs. McKinney had decided to homeschool Lillie. In hindsight, they wondered if they had protected her
too much.

All in the name of love.

Love was a word Dawson rarely used. Never in conjunc-
tion with his mother or his missing father. Hearing it asso-
ciated with Lillie's name gave him pause. Surely, the way
he felt about the pretty secretary wasn't love. Or was it?
He thought of her kiss and the way she had molded into
his embrace.

As much as he enjoyed kissing her, he didn't like the
turmoil of emotion that welled up within him today. Plus,
Lillie had pulled away from him last night, so she must be
equally confused.

More than anything, she needed closure, which Dawson
hoped would come when all the facts about her mother's
death were brought to light.

Dawson hadn't told Mr. McKinney about his own personal involvement in the case. Eventually, the two men who
cared about Lillie would have another heart-to-heart talk.
Although after learning the truth, Mr. McKinney might not
want to ever see Dawson again.

His phone rang. He grabbed the cell off the kitchen
counter and smiled when he saw Lillie's name on the caller
ID.

"I'm sorry about what my father said this morning," she
said in greeting.

"It's okay, Lillie."

"He's really a good man, who thinks the best of people.
That's why I'm not sure where that comment came from."

"He's worried about you. We shared a pot of decaf last night after you went to bed."

"Oh? Then maybe fatigue was playing into the mix this morning."

Dawson laughed, although when he thought of the cozy farmhouse and her loving parents, he had a pang of regret. Lillie would soon be going to church with her parents. He wanted to be sitting next to her in the pew.

"Something's troubling you," Lillie said as if she could sense his mood. "It's more than my father's comment. You haven't been yourself since you visited the prison yesterday."

"I'm okay."

"I'm sure seeing where Granger had been incarcerated made everything real."

"It was real before, Lillie."

"But you hadn't experienced it firsthand."

He leaned against the counter in the kitchen. "I've been in jails before."

"You came face-to-face with who he was, or who you thought he was, and it hit you. Hard. Then my father's comment this morning drove home the point even more so."

She was right, although he wasn't ready to admit the way his gut had twisted when the door to the cell block closed behind them. Stepping into the prison where his father had lived for fifteen years had affected him, and not in a good way.

"As you told Karl Nelson," Lillie continued, "your father's trial was a sham. He wasn't guilty."

"All we know is that the blood on the shirt wasn't his, Lillie. That's different than being completely exonerated."

"But if Granger had been guilty, he wouldn't have come back to Freemont."

"Perpetrators often return to the scene of their crime."

She let out a frustrated sigh. "Granger was searching

for information and was murdered because of what he uncovered."

Dawson nodded. "You're right."

"Of course I am. You and I saw the videos. We heard his
voice and watched as he looked over his shoulder, fearful
that the killer was after him."

"We don't know who was after him," Dawson corrected
her. "Granger could have made enemies in prison who
sought him out once he was released. Cons have friends
on the outside who do their bidding. The only thing we do
know for sure is that my father was released from prison,
and someone came after him. Besides, Lillie, I was more
upset about the prison per se, not that my father had been
held there."

"I don't understand."

"The four walls seemed to crowd me in."

"You told me you didn't like confined spaces."

He wanted to change the subject, but Lillie refused to
let it drop.

She pulled in a sharp breath. "Did...did something happen? Your mother—"

Sensing her concern, he held up his hand as if she could
see his nonverbal gesture. "Nothing like that. No abuse. No
locked closets with me inside, if that's what you're thinking."

As much as he didn't want to tell her, Lillie deserved
to know. "I worked summer construction jobs during high
school."

"Following in your father's footsteps."

Intuitively he knew she was right, but he couldn't admit
the truth. "I worked construction because it provided good
money. Not because of Granger Ford."

"Are you sure?"

"Of course I'm sure." He pulled away from the counter
and stepped toward the window. The sun was hidden from

view by a line of clouds. "I was on the job late, finishing a ditch. Must have been seven or eight feet deep and just wide enough for the main sewer pipe. The earth started to crumble. Before I could get out, the sides collapsed, trapping me under a huge mound of dirt."

The memory of being buried alive swept over him again. He was surrounded by the cloying scent of the Georgia clay that blocked the daylight and sucked air from his lungs.

He shuddered, trying to shake off the memory.

Don't look back, an interior voice warned.

Sweat dampened his neck.

Lillie's voice came to him like a warm touch on a cold day. "You survived, Dawson."

"Yeah." He laughed ruefully. "Thanks to the men who dug me out."

"Did your dad know what happened?"

"Of course not."

She sighed. "Ironic that neither of us knew our fathers."

"But it doesn't seem to bother you."

"I never knew my birth father. My foster father was a good man. He filled the empty role."

"What about your foster mother?"

"I…I always held something back, which was probably a self-protective measure, because I didn't want to be hurt again."

Lillie's voice was almost devoid of emotion. He imagined the firm set of her jaw and her braced shoulders. She had her own painful memories from the past, maybe more than she was willing to admit.

Silence filled the line until she finally spoke again. "I…I found something when I was online this morning. It probably doesn't have any bearing on this case, but you said sometimes the smallest item can be important."

"That's right."

"I searched for missing women in the surrounding small towns. I only looked at the month of January."

"What'd you find?"

"Valerie Taylor went missing ten years ago and was last seen on Saturday of the MLK weekend that year. Roseanne Manning disappeared the same weekend."

"Lots of women go missing, Lillie."

"Roseanne was from Millsville, Georgia, which isn't far from Freemont."

"And Valerie?"

"She lived in Culpepper."

Dawson pursed his lips. "Interesting."

"But probably doesn't mean anything."

He glanced at his watch. "Don't you have to get ready for church?"

Lillie laughed. "Sounds like you're trying to get rid of me."

"I'll call you later."

After they hung up, Dawson kept thinking about Lillie's foster family. Being with her parents had made him realize the hole in his own heart and the desire he'd always had to live the kind of life she had known.

Both he and Lillie approached relationships with caution, as if they lived under a yellow stoplight. Most folks rode through life on green, going full steam ahead and never glancing over their shoulders. In comparison, Lillie and Dawson weighed where they were going in relation to where they had been.

He envisioned her sitting in the pew at church and then at the potluck lunch after the service. In his mind's eye, he saw a line of farm boys, bulked up from baling hay, falling over themselves to refill her sweet tea or bring her another slice of Mrs. McKinney's chocolate cake.

Dawson let out a ragged breath. He was being irrational,

but no matter how much he tried to focus on other things, he kept thinking about her emerald eyes and full lips, lips he had kissed last night and wanted to kiss again.

He changed into his running clothes and hit the trails around Fort Rickman. The fresh air cleared his mind and pushed aside the crazy thoughts about the country suitors. As soon as he was back at his apartment, he showered and changed and headed through the main gate and back to Lillie's house.

He had good reason to return, he kept telling himself, even as he stood on her porch and saw the surprised look on her face when she opened the front door.

"I decided to visit the town of Millsville, where Roseanne Manning was last seen before she disappeared. I wondered if you felt like taking a drive."

"I'll get my purse and tell my mother we'll be back later."

With Lillie sitting next to him, Dawson's mood lightened. "How was the potluck?" he asked, as if he hadn't been thinking about it nonstop.

"I ate too much." She laughed. "And ran into a lot of folks I hadn't seen in a while."

"Some of the local farmers?"

She nodded. "Mainly I talked to my mother's friends. The folks my age have moved away from the area."

"Probably a few single guys hanging around." As much as he didn't want to seem needy, the words sprang from his mouth.

"No one of interest."

"Really?"

"Of course Jermaine Daniels was there. We had cake and ice cream together."

Dawson's optimism plummeted. "Nice guy?"

"One of the best." Her lips twitched and her eyes twinkled with the laughter she tried to contain.

"What's so funny?" He felt as if he'd missed the punch line of a joke.

"Jermaine is ten years old and the cutest kid in the area." She poked Dawson in the ribs.

He grabbed her hand and laughed. "Okay, so I was thinking about all the men hovering around your table."

"You sound jealous."

"Of course not." But when he looked at her, he knew he was easy to read. "You're right. I was jealous."

"Jermaine's the only one you need to worry about, and I think you can handle a ten-year-old."

He continued to smile, enjoying her playful banter and the sun that peeked out from behind the clouds.

Their Sunday drive ended when they pulled into Millsville, a sleepy crossroads that appeared to be in hibernation.

The only cars were those parked on the grass around the AME church, where a cluster of men stood talking. The women gathered to the side, dressed in their Sunday finest, including large-brimmed hats in deep russets and reds that accentuated their dark skin.

Dawson helped Lillie from the car. "You talk to the ladies, and I'll see what the gentlemen remember."

The men were friendly and grateful someone was looking into the case of the missing eighteen-year-old. "Roseanne was an attractive child with a wandering spirit. She claimed Atlanta was where she was meant to live."

"Do folks think she left town on her own?"

One of the men shook his head and tsked. "We don't know. Most think something happened to her. Something bad. Her mama died of a broken heart not long after the child disappeared. She never had a daddy, at least not one that stayed around."

Dawson felt his own gut tighten. He could relate.

"When was Roseanne last seen?"

"Martin Luther King Day, ten years ago. She was hanging around some red-haired man from a neighboring town."

The lazy Sunday turned sour. "Anyone recall the guy's name, or do you remember what he looked like? Anything that would make him stand out from the crowd?"

"His hair," one man said, causing the others to nod in agreement. "And the scar on his right cheek."

"What about Valerie Taylor, from Culpepper, south of here. Does her name sound familiar?"

An older man rubbed his jaw and nodded. "Matter a fact, Val and Roseanne were friends. The girls did everything together."

Lillie and Dawson met up at the car. Her eyes were wide as she climbed inside. "I've got something."

Dawson waved goodbye to the church folks before he pulled onto the roadway. "Okay, what?"

"Roseanne had been seeing a boy from Freemont."

"Red hair?" Dawson asked.

Lillie pointed to her own face. "He had a scar on his right cheek and his name was Everett."

"What's that tell you?"

"Billy Everett may be our killer."

"Guess who Roseanne's good friend was?"

Lillie dropped her jaw. "Valerie Taylor?"

"You got that right."

Heading back to the McKinney farm, Dawson felt a weight lift from his shoulders. Billy Everett seemed to be in the middle of this case no matter where they turned. Finally something was paying off. Plus, Dawson planned to clear the air completely with the McKinneys and tell them who his father really was.

A car Lillie didn't recognize was parked in the driveway when Dawson pulled to a stop in front of the farmhouse. He followed her inside and helped her with her coat, which she hung in the hall closet.

Motioning him forward, she headed through the living room with Dawson close behind. "Mother? Dad?"

"We're in the kitchen, dear." Her mother's voice.

As Dawson entered the airy room, a man sitting with Walter and Sarah shoved his chair back from the table.

"Nice to see you again, Agent Timmons." Sergeant Ron Pritchard rose to his feet. "I was talking to the McKinneys about what's been happening in Freemont. Seems you didn't tell them everything about the murder case."

Lillie took a step forward. "Officer Pritchard, please."

Mr. McKinney stared at Dawson. "Granger Ford caused Lillie enough pain. I don't want her to be hurt again."

"Sir, I can explain everything." Dawson turned to Pritchard. "Why did you come here?"

"I wanted to know if Granger had contacted them." Pritchard smiled at Lillie's parents. "Nice talking to you folks. I'll see myself out."

Dawson opened the front door for the cop and followed him onto the porch. "You've got bad timing."

Pritchard raised his brow. "At least I tell the truth."

"What's that supposed to mean?"

"You weren't forthright, Agent Timmons. Why didn't you tell me Granger Ford was your father? We contacted the prison to see if he had any family. He had listed you as his next of kin."

Pritchard walked toward his car, then, pausing to glance at Dawson, he nodded. "Have a nice day."

Dawson turned to go back into the house. Mr. McKinney stood in the doorway, his eyes narrowed, his mouth pulled into a tight line.

"Maybe you should leave now, young man."

"Sir, I need to ensure Lillie's all right."

"I can take care of my daughter. You head back to Fort Rickman and don't come around here again."

"Sir—"

The door closed and the lock slid into place.

Dawson stood on the porch for a long moment before he hustled back to his car. Mr. McKinney was right. Lillie didn't need an ex-con's son in her life. Especially an ex-con who might have killed her biological mother. How could he and Lillie have a future together when their pasts revolved around a murder?

Now a killer was on the loose.

Although Dawson was committed to keeping Lillie safe, her father—with his arsenal of guns and his awards for marksmanship—would have to protect her tonight.

THIRTEEN

"I'm sorry, Dawson."

Lillie sat next to him as he drove her back to Fort Rickman the next morning. He had called last night and arranged to pick her up bright and early.

"My father reacted without thinking," she said. "He's a good man but extremely protective. Plus, he's worried about me."

She tugged at a wayward strand of hair. "Which is exactly why I didn't want either my mother or father to know about Granger's death."

Dawson tightened his grip on the steering wheel. "In my opinion, Pritchard is a jerk."

"He questioned them about my birth mother's death and the trial. He also wanted to know how they heard about me after my mother disappeared."

"What did they tell him?"

"One of the men from church mentioned a child in need. My mother was a retired schoolteacher. It didn't take long before they were awarded custody."

"Do you know anything about when you first arrived at their house?"

"Only that I didn't talk for a number of weeks. When I finally did speak, I refused to mention my birth mother.

They soon realized I had blacked out everything, except the memory of that night in the storm."

"What about the man's voice?"

"They heard me screaming from my bedroom one night and found me huddled in the corner. I told them not to let the man close the door."

"Your mother's house burned to the ground?"

She nodded. "Not long after she disappeared."

"Was anything salvaged?"

"Only a few trinkets my foster mother boxed up for me." Lillie gazed out the window and settled back in the seat.

Dawson seemed equally lost in his own thoughts until he pulled to a stop in the driveway of her Freemont home. "I'll wait out here while you change for work." He reached for his cell. "Pack a bag for a couple nights. I'll make a reservation for you at the Lodge."

"I'd really like to stay in my own home."

"I know, but we've talked about this before. Your safety comes first."

Lillie smiled and the day brightened. "Actually, I'm grateful you're concerned about me."

While she was inside, he called the Lodge and reserved two rooms—one for Lillie, and one for himself across the hall so he could keep watch over her room throughout the night.

She reappeared, carrying her bag. Dawson met her on the sidewalk and helped her into his car, placing her case behind her seat.

By the time they arrived at Fort Rickman, traffic jammed the entrance to post. Soldiers who lived off post were heading to their early-morning physical training, and the long line of cars snaked slowly through the main gate checkpoints.

"Join me for lunch?" Dawson asked when he parked in front of post headquarters.

"I usually work at my desk through the noon hour, but I could make an exception today."

"What about dinner instead?" he asked. "I'll cook. Although don't expect anything too elaborate. I'm a meat and potatoes type of guy."

"I'll like whatever you serve. Plus I'm willing to help."

She hustled toward the front of the headquarters and turned to wave at him before going inside.

He headed back to his BOQ to shower and change. What would happen today was important and could alter the future of his military career. If Pritchard had uncovered Dawson's relationship to Granger Ford, the CID would be able to as well.

Better to be proactive and let the chief know right away, just as Dawson had wanted to do on Friday. The last thing he needed was for Wilson to hear the news from someone else.

Entering CID headquarters, Dawson nodded to Corporal Otis, who manned the front desk. "How's it going, Ray?"

"Ah, sir, the chief wants to see you in his office."

"Now?"

"He said as soon as you arrive."

The look on the corporal's face wasn't encouraging. "Anything I should know?"

"You know what I know, sir."

Dawson headed for the chief's office. He rapped three times and opened the door when he heard Wilson's command to enter.

"Morning, Chief." He nodded to Wilson before he noticed the commanding general, sitting in a chair to the right of Wilson's desk. "Sir."

"Come in, Agent Timmons." Wilson motioned him forward. "General Cameron and I have some questions about Granger Ford's death in relation to Lillie Beaumont."

Dawson quickly filled both the chief and the commanding general in on the investigation and the information Granger had saved on the flash drive. He told them about Leonard Simpson and his parents and about the college boy in the bar as well as the three Atlanta women and two younger girls who had gone missing over various MLK weekends.

"I know it sounds somewhat complicated, sirs, but I feel confident the person who killed Granger Ford also killed Lillie's mother. Right now, a man named Billy Everett is of interest. The Freemont police are looking for him."

"You've kept Sergeant Pritchard apprised of what you've found?" Wilson asked.

Dawson swallowed. "Not everything, sir."

"Oh?"

"I wanted to check out the information on the flash drive first."

"Which you did Friday night."

"Yes, sir."

"Then you and Ms. Beaumont drove to Atlanta on Saturday to confirm what Granger had revealed on the video."

Dawson nodded. "Yes, sir."

"And you saw Pritchard that evening as you returned to Freemont, yet you were still less than forthright about what you had uncovered."

"Sergeant Pritchard did not indicate he wanted to share information at that time, sir."

Wilson raised his brow. "Perhaps because you had the flash drive."

"Roger that, sir."

"What did Special Agent Jamison Steele tell you on Friday morning about the investigation?"

"Excuse me?"

Wilson splayed his hands on his desk. "Agent Steele told you to protect Ms. Beaumont and leave the investigation to the Freemont police."

A muscle in Dawson's neck twitched. "Ah, yes, sir. That's correct."

"Yet you proceeded with the investigation."

"I was confirming information I had received, sir."

"What is your relationship to Granger Ford?"

"Sir, he—" Dawson let out a ragged breath. "Anecdotally, I believe he is my father."

"Anecdotally?"

"Yes, sir. His name is not on my birth certificate, but my mother claims he was my father. He was never in my life. In fact, I first talked to him over the phone only a few days before his death, and I never met him face-to-face."

Wilson nodded. "I spoke briefly with Agent Steele this morning. He said you were concerned about your military paperwork because of that very issue."

"That's correct, sir, but I want to assure you Agent Steele did not know about the flash drive or my trip to Atlanta."

Wilson sat back in his chair and tapped his pencil on his desk. "Why didn't you inform Agent Steele?"

"We're severely understaffed, and he was tied up on other cases. I didn't want to pull him away from his own investigations."

Wilson nodded, then turned to the commanding general. "Sir, is there anything you would like to ask Agent Timmons?"

"Ms. Beaumont expressed her concern that the investigation could adversely affect the funding drive for the new museum on post," the general said.

"Yes, sir. She expressed those same concerns to me as well."

"Have you uncovered anything that would paint Fort Rickman in a negative light or anything that would tarnish the military's stellar reputation in south Georgia?"

"No, sir."

"You will continue to ensure Ms. Beaumont's safety?"

"That has my highest priority, General Cameron."

"Excellent."

Chief Wilson raked his hand over his jaw and eyed Dawson before saying, "I expect a full report on my desk by Wednesday afternoon. Share the information you've uncovered with Sergeant Pritchard. He's in charge of this investigation."

"Yes, sir."

"I'll talk to the Judge Advocate General's Corps on post and ask them to review your military file. I don't have to tell you, Dawson, if JAG determines you falsified military records, it could mean the end of your career."

"I understand, sir."

Dawson left the chief's office with a heavy weight on his chest, knowing his time in the CID could be coming to an end. He had told the general that Lillie was top priority, which she was, but finding her mother's killer was the best way Dawson knew to keep her safe. Once the killer was brought to justice, Lillie would be able to return to her own home and the life she had lived before Granger's death. Where would Dawson fit into the mix?

Hopefully not fighting his own court battles about fraudulent military records. Ironic that he could be found guilty just as his father had been. Dawson had never thought Granger Ford's misfortune with the law would rub off on him.

Lillie looked up as Karl Nelson entered the general's suite, briefcase in hand. "Good morning, sir."

"How are you, Lillie?"

"Fine, sir, but I'm afraid General Cameron hasn't arrived yet this morning."

The aide glanced up from his computer. "The general's at CID headquarters."

Which Mark hadn't mentioned earlier. Concern tugged at Lillie. What was General Cameron doing with the CID? Surely it didn't have anything to do with Dawson.

"I'll wait until the general arrives." The construction contractor took a seat on the couch, the same couch Lillie had slept on two nights ago. She noted the afghan needed to be folded and walked over to readjust the throw.

"May I get you some coffee, Mr. Nelson?"

He held open his hand. "Two cups in the morning is max for me, Lillie, so I'll have to say no. Any chance I could spread out the plans for the museum before the general arrives? I want him to see the updated design that just came back from the architect."

"There's a table in the conference room."

Karl followed her along the back hallway and stopped in front of the museum model. "Beautiful, isn't it?" His full face beamed with pride.

"Yes, sir. It will be a wonderful facility for both the military and civilian communities."

"General Cameron and I plan to name one of the rooms after my dad. He worked diligently throughout his lifetime to help the military."

"That would be a perfect tribute to your father's memory."

Karl smiled. "Thank you for saying so. I'm not sure if folks understand my need to perpetuate his good name."

"Maybe they've never lost a loved one who worked so hard to make the world a better place."

"I appreciate that, Lillie. You're probably right."

When General Cameron returned to headquarters, Lillie directed him into the conference area, where he shook hands with Karl.

Wanting to find out why the general had been at CID headquarters, she slipped back to her desk and called Dawson's cell phone. When he failed to answer, she left a message.

Pinpricks of anxiety rumbled along her spine. She shouldn't be worried, but she was.

Pritchard couldn't be trusted to keep the information about Dawson's dad to himself. The CID had probably been notified.

Hopefully the disclosure wouldn't adversely affect Dawson's career. His father had been released from prison because of an inaccurate blood test. Many folks would probably wonder if he should have remained behind bars, just as Karl Nelson had mentioned the day of the shooting.

By the time the contractor and the general finished their meeting, Lillie still hadn't heard from Dawson.

The general escorted the civilian into the outer office. "The sooner you can get the construction completed, Karl, the better."

"My feelings exactly, General. Now that the donations are starting to pour in, I'm feeling even more optimistic. If everything goes according to plan, the museum should be ready to occupy by summer. Just so you know, I've restricted access to the site for safety reasons and instructed my crew to start working on the foundation as soon as possible. As much rain as we've had recently, I want to take advantage of every good day."

"I agree. The ceremony on Wednesday is to build enthusiasm for the project and garner more funding. We'll hold an even bigger celebration when the building is completed."

The general turned to Lillie. "Have we gotten many RSVPs back yet?"

"Yes, sir. More than forty guests will be in the special seating area. Bleachers will be available for folks from town and the surrounding area."

Karl nodded his approval, then winked at Lillie before he turned back to the general. "I hope Lillie and Mark will be able to attend."

The general smiled. "Everyone in headquarters will be there."

After shaking hands, the general returned to his office. Before the construction company owner opened the outer door, he hesitated. "I'm happy you're working here, Lillie, and doing so well for yourself. I never knew your mother, but I always regretted that Nelson Construction equipment played a role in her death."

Lillie appreciated the older man's words. "At least her body was recovered." She paused, thinking of the names on the flash drive. "I fear there might be other women who have suffered the same demise, yet they'll never be found and their families will always wonder what happened to them."

Karl nodded, his face drawn. "There's so much sorrow in the world these days. Even within families. Sometimes the person we know best can cause us the most pain. Human nature is hard to understand. I was fortunate. My dad was a great man. He lived a life of virtue, the way I try to live mine." Karl pursed his full lips. "Big shoes to fill. I'm just glad the museum will be a lasting reminder of the man he really was."

Lillie wished she could remember her own mother in such a positive way. Just as Karl had said, those closest to a person often caused the most pain. Growing up, Lillie had thought she had done something wrong that had made her mother abandon her.

Although she hadn't told Dawson, Lillie had never looked in the box of her mother's mementos that had been saved from the fire. Secretly, she feared it would contain proof her mother hadn't loved her.

By noon, Lillie knew what she had to do. She told Mark she'd be back later and headed for her car. In the parking lot, she met up with the bodybuilder manager from the Freemont gym.

Tom Reynolds greeted her with a warm smile. "Mark's taking me to the post fitness center to work on a reciprocal membership for military personnel with our facility in town."

"Good for you, Tom."

He shrugged off the praise. "Actually, Karl Nelson came up with the idea. He's always trying to help the army guys and gals."

"Karl was here earlier but didn't mention anything about the gym agreement."

"Probably because he's so focused on the new museum."

"He did say donations have been pouring in, which makes all of us happy."

"You'll be at the ceremony Wednesday?" Tom asked.

"I wouldn't miss it."

Once off post, Lillie grabbed her cell phone and left a message for Dawson.

"I can't meet you for lunch. There's something at my house I need to get, which shouldn't take long. Don't worry. I'll be fine."

As she drove through Freemont, dark clouds appeared overhead. She needed to hurry so she could get back to headquarters before the rain started to fall.

Pulling into her driveway, she felt a sense of relief, as if everything had been blown out of proportion. No one had followed her. She could make a quick stop and be back on post within the hour.

She entered through the front door, wanting to return to her normal life, and shoved thoughts of what had happened aside. Walking purposefully through her living room, she continued on into the hallway where she had huddled on stormy nights, just as that little girl had so long ago. A little girl who'd grown up thinking she had done something wrong.

Lillie now knew she could face the truth about the past. She was a stronger woman. She believed in God's mercy and knew He was always with her and would ensure she wouldn't be harmed no matter what she found.

After opening her bedroom closet, she pushed aside the shoe boxes stacked on the shelf filled with off-season shoes, sandals and strappy pumps she wore on warmer days. Stretching on tiptoe, she touched the wooden box in the back of the closet.

Swallowing down a lump of apprehension, she dusted off the top with her hand and placed the box on the edge of her bed. Lillie drew in a fortifying breath before she lifted the lid. Her heart warmed when she looked inside.

The box contained a few pieces of jewelry, not the fake costume jewelry that Lillie usually wore, but what appeared to be expensive items. She held up a strand of fine pearls, perfectly matched and brilliant in color, along with a gold bracelet and matching necklace.

On the underside of the bracelet, she noticed "14K" etched in the precious metal. Both gold pieces were weighty and would cost a small fortune in today's economy.

A tiny gift card was tucked under the jewelry. She opened the note and rubbed her finger across the swirl of ink. The script was bold and the letters perfectly formed.

"To my precious Irene. I am forever yours."

Had the note and the jewelry been gifts from the man Lillie heard in her dreams?

Returning to the box, she pulled out a brooch in the shape of an American flag, set with red, white and blue rhinestones. Another gift, perhaps?

Toward the bottom was a piece of construction paper she unfolded. A child's drawing. Someone had written along the top, *My adorable Lillie is such an artist,* and the date, just a few days before her mother disappeared.

Hot tears swarmed Lillie's eyes. Unable to control her emotions, she lowered her head to her hands and cried for the mother's love she had lost too early. For a life cut short. For her own mistake in thinking her mother had purposely left her alone on that stormy night so long ago.

The tears were cathartic. Maybe now she would be able to reach out to her foster mother without fear of being left again.

Lillie clutched the brooch and held it to her heart. Her mother's body had been found along the river, not far from the museum construction site. Wearing the brooch to the military ceremony on Wednesday would be a fitting and patriotic tribute to honor her mother, whom Lillie had closed out of her heart for too long.

She dabbed tissues to her eyes and blew her nose. Then, grabbing the note and drawing to show Dawson, she stuck both papers in her purse. As she started to stand, she noticed a man's cuff link, partially broken, wedged in the bottom of the wooden container.

Lillie held it up, trying to determine the initials set in gold. The first letter was almost completely missing, but the second looked like the letter *T. GT,* perhaps, for Georgia Tech?

A bolt of lightning brightened the day. Thunder cracked, so strong it took her breath away. Her heart stopped for a long moment. She closed the box and jammed it in her closet.

Her stomach roiled. An odor wafted past her and mixed with the earthy, musky scent of the approaching rain.

Fear threaded through her veins.

She couldn't hide from the storm or from the smell of smoke. Lightning must have struck her house.

"Fire," she wanted to scream.

Another crash of thunder.

Unable to move forward, she huddled on the floor. As

on that night so long ago, she saw the door to her mother's room and heard the man's voice closing her out.

"No!" she screamed.

"Lillie." Dawson's voice sounded above the thunder. He wrapped her in his arms and guided her outside.

A portion of her garage was scorched. A pile of smoldering pine straw had been pushed away from the structure.

Glancing up, she saw that someone had written terrible slurs and disparaging names with spray paint across the side of her garage. Why hadn't she noticed them earlier when she had parked in the driveway?

Lillie looked at Dawson, not understanding what had happened. "The lightning hit the house?"

He shook his head. "It wasn't lightning. Someone used gasoline. I must have scared him off before the fire took hold. The water hose was close by."

Suddenly things weren't making sense. "How…how did you know…?"

"You left a message on my phone."

She glanced at her own cell. "But you didn't return my call."

"I was driving as fast as I could, Lillie. Why did you come back here? I told you to be careful."

Lillie pulled something from her pocket. Opening her hand, she looked down at the broken cuff link with the letters she had thought were *GT* for Georgia Tech. In the light of day, she realized the second letter could be an *F*.

Dawson had arrived just as the fire had started. Or had he started the fire to convince her she was in danger?

"I'll call the police and let them know what happened," she said, digging in her purse for her cell.

He shook his head, his eyes dark. "The fire's out. We need to get back to post, where you'll be safe. I'll call Pritchard on the way."

A feeling of dread swept over her. Her ears rang a warning as she glanced down at the cuff link.

GF. Granger Ford.

He wasn't her mother's lover. Lillie knew that without a shadow of a doubt. But he could have been her killer.

Dawson was his father's son. Karl Nelson's words returned to haunt her. *"Often the people we know best are the people who cause us the most pain."*

Lillie had thought she could trust the CID agent, but she was wrong. Dawson had started the fire to prove his point about her need for safety.

Since Granger was dead, if someone came after Lillie, people would think the killer was still on the loose.

Which is exactly what Lillie had thought.

Now she wasn't sure who was trying to do her harm—a killer from the past, or a CID agent who seemed intent on clearing his father's tarnished name?

Dawson followed Lillie back to post and knew she was upset about more than just the storm. She hadn't told him why she had gone back to her house, but he wasn't blind and had noticed the patriotic brooch she had pinned to her jacket.

The pin looked old and valuable. Maybe it had belonged to Mrs. McKinney. Or Lillie could have bought it for herself. Then again, maybe an old boyfriend had given it to her as a gift. Dawson rubbed his right hand over his chin, trying not to envision Lillie with someone else.

Surely there had been a line of men who wanted to court the pretty secretary, especially with all the single soldiers stationed on an army post. Had there been a very special person in her past? Maybe someone still in the military? Deployed? Returning soon?

The more he considered the options, the more confused he became. He hadn't seen photographs of a guy displayed in her home or on her desk at work. But with digital photography, most folks kept their pictures on their computers. While she was asleep the other night, he could have opened her photo file.

Then he'd know.

Although in reality, he didn't want to know about any guys, and he would never intrude upon her privacy. What he was interested in was her safety and getting to the bottom of this investigation. Then both of them would go their separate ways. The thought of not seeing Lillie sent another wave of frustration that tightened his shoulders into a knot.

Dawson reached for his cell and called the Freemont police. Once Sergeant Pritchard was on the line, Dawson filled him in on the fire and the graffiti written on Lillie's garage.

"I'm escorting Ms. Beaumont back to post." Dawson glanced at his watch. "I'll meet you at her house in thirty minutes. We need to talk."

By the time he pulled into the post headquarters parking lot, she was already on the sidewalk headed toward the building.

"Lillie?" he called after her.

She glanced over her shoulder.

"Are we still on for dinner tonight?"

"I can't, Dawson. I have too much work to do."

"You've got a room at the Lodge," he reminded her, knowing how vulnerable she'd be if she returned to her house.

"I'll stay at the Lodge, but I won't be available for dinner." With that very definite rejection, she hurried up the steps and into the building.

Dawson jammed a fist into his hand. How had things changed so quickly between them?

He thought back to what had happened earlier. She'd been frightened by the thunder and had readily accepted his open arms as he'd helped her outside. Was she upset because he hadn't called her on the way? A niggling voice that he couldn't explain had insisted he needed to hurry. He hadn't even thought about phoning her.

His mistake.

A mistake that seemed to have made a difference with Lillie. With so many things stacked between them, no wonder she wanted to call a halt to spending time together.

Her dad had probably talked to her yesterday. He was worried about her safety and rightfully so. Dawson was as well.

Only Dawson wasn't the one she needed to fear. He glanced at the cars driving by the headquarters building. Someone was out there, waiting for Lillie.

Even if she didn't want his help, he would do everything to ensure she remained safe. Hopefully the case would break soon so Lillie could go on with her life.

He didn't want to say goodbye to Lillie. Not tomorrow or the next day or the day after that. Maybe not ever.

FOURTEEN

Sergeant Pritchard and two of his officers were searching the area around Lillie's garage when Dawson parked in her driveway. Pulling in a deep breath, he stepped onto the pavement.

After instructing his men to keep searching, Pritchard brushed off his hands and approached Dawson. "Looks like the killer may have returned to the scene of the crime."

"Lillie was inside at the time. I arrived just as the pine straw started to ignite. He must have run off into the woods."

"Did you see anyone?"

Dawson shook his head. "I barely had time to grab the water hose and douse the flames."

"Had Ms. Beaumont heard anything?"

"Thunder rumbled overhead, which probably drowned out any noise he might have made."

The cop held up two fingers. "The killer dropped the boulder on your car Saturday night and tried to burn her house today. Anything else I should know about?"

Dawson explained about the key Granger had given Lillie, and the SUV that had tried to run her off the road and then followed her in Freemont.

"We found a flash drive that had information Granger had uncovered, along with two videos he made shortly before his death. He wanted to get the information into the right hands in case something happened to him."

Pritchard narrowed his eyes. "You didn't think I should know about the information?"

"I wanted to ensure it was accurate. That's why we went to Atlanta on Saturday." Dawson explained about meeting with Leonard Simpson and his parents.

The cop scratched his head. "Seems a stretch to think three prostitutes in Atlanta could tie in with Irene Beaumont's death."

"Which is exactly why I wanted to ensure the information was accurate before I handed it off to you."

Pritchard seemed to accept the explanation. "You still should have told me about your relationship to Granger Ford."

"You're right, but at the time I wasn't ready to accept the fact myself. I'd closed him out of my life for so long and couldn't find the gumption to acknowledge he was my father."

Pritchard looked into the distance and let out a ragged breath. "I don't condone what you did, but I understand. Fact is, I never got along with my old man. He was a mean buzzard who hurt a lot of people, including my mother. If I found him dead on someone's doorstep, I'd walk over his body and never look down. No way would I claim he was kin."

Dawson appreciated the cop's candor. It was hard to admit bad blood in a family, especially when the family member was your dad. He continued to fill Pritchard in on what he had uncovered as well as the two local women who had been seen with Billy Everett. "His name keeps popping up."

"I'll send out another BOLO for law enforcement in Georgia and the surrounding states to be on the lookout for Everett."

"Sounds good. As soon as I get back to my office, I'll email the flash drive files to you."

The two men shook hands before Dawson climbed into his car and drove back to post. He and Pritchard had ironed out their differences, and Dawson felt sure they would be able to work together in the future.

Once at his desk, he sent Pritchard the files and then placed a call to the guidance counselor at the local high school.

"She's tied up with testing this afternoon," her secretary said.

"Would you have her call me when she's free?" Dawson asked. "I'm interested in Freemont High graduates who attended Georgia Tech twenty-five to thirty years ago."

"Records that old might be difficult to access." The secretary stated the obvious.

"Please, just pass on the request."

He left his name and phone number. Hopefully the counselor would return his call later in the day.

Wanting to update the chief, Dawson tapped on Wilson's door.

"Enter."

"Sir, I met with Sergeant Pritchard and brought him up to date. He sent out a BOLO on Billy Everett, who, at the present time, is our only suspect. The Freemont police will keep us posted if anything new develops."

"Sounds good."

Dawson hesitated before finally asking, "Sir, have you heard anything from JAG?"

"Not yet. I'll let you know when I do."

"Yes, sir."

Dawson wasn't encouraged when he left the chief's office. Everything seemed to be moving at a snail's pace, and he was hanging in thin air when it came to Lillie and what the JAG Corps would determine. Dawson wanted the case resolved as soon as possible. Then he'd try to figure out his future, knowing without Lillie, the future looked anything but bright.

Lillie hurried into her office, determined to review the files on Granger's flash drive. Dawson had been with her when she'd watched the video the first time. Feigning concern, the solicitous CID agent had even suggested she *not* watch the tape, which made her wonder if there was something Dawson hadn't wanted her to see.

Thinking back to that night, Lillie remembered her own internal struggle and how often she'd turned away from the screen unable to go on. What had she missed?

She opened the bottom drawer on her desk where she had placed the flash drive, but the memory device wasn't there. She searched through all the drawers. A cold suspicion took hold that Dawson had taken the flash drive without telling her.

Lillie reached for her phone and tapped in his number.

"Timmons."

His voice made her heart hitch, but she pushed aside the feeling. She had to be careful. Things weren't always as they seemed and right now she couldn't trust anyone. Especially not Dawson.

"I wanted to relook at the files on the flash drive we viewed the other night, but I couldn't find it in my desk. Did you take it?"

"You put it in the bottom drawer."

Which was the first place she had looked.

"Are you sure you don't have the flash drive?" she asked again.

"Lillie, I don't know what happened today, but I'm not the bad guy. You can believe me when I tell you something.

I don't have the flash drive. However, I did forward the files to my computer. I can email you a copy if that would help."

"Have you deleted anything?"

"Lillie, where's this coming from? Did your father tell you to not trust me?"

Her father had cautioned her to be careful, but he'd also said he liked Dawson. His main concern was for her own peace of mind. Eventually, he had told her to trust her instincts, which she was trying to do.

"Just send me the files, Dawson."

As she hung up, Mark entered the office. He stopped, noting the papers and other items scattered over the top of her usually neat desk.

"What's wrong?"

She waved her hand in the air, hoping to make light of the situation. "I can't find a flash drive. I thought it was in my desk. Have you seen one lying around? It's small, eight gigs, encased in blue enamel."

He shook his head. "But I'll let you know if I find it."

"Was anyone hanging around the office this morning?"

"Tom Reynolds stopped by. He wanted to talk to me about the gym on post."

"Did he touch anything on my desk?"

"Of course not." Mark pursed his lips. "I came in late Saturday morning and found Sergeant Howard Murphy looking out the window. He was the staff duty NCO and thought he saw the general's car in the parking lot."

"General Cameron was out of town for the weekend, Mark. You knew his schedule, so why were you here?"

The aide glanced down. "I got behind last week and wanted to catch up on some paperwork. The NCO said you and the CID agent had stayed at the office Friday night."

"Dawson didn't think it was safe for me to return home.

I've got a room at the Lodge for the next two days. He assures me I'll be safer on post."

Mark nodded. "He's probably right. I'll be working late tonight. Call me if you have a problem. The Lodge isn't far. I could get there in no time."

Lillie appreciated his offer. The cocky aide seemed to have come back down to earth. She felt better knowing he would be close at hand.

When she checked into her room at the Lodge later that afternoon, Lillie knew she had a long night ahead of her. The last time she had opened Granger's files, Dawson had been at her side, offering support. Only now she couldn't depend on him, and just like when she was growing up, the only one she could depend on was herself.

FIFTEEN

Dawson wanted to knock on the door to Lillie's room at the Lodge and demand to know what was bothering her. She had given him more than the cold shoulder earlier. In fact, he'd call it an arctic freeze. But bottom line, she didn't want him around right now, so whether he liked it or not, he needed to give her space.

The room he had reserved for Lillie was at the end of a long hallway on the second floor, away from the central stairway and other guests who might be going to and from their rooms. Dawson holed up across the hall with the door to his room cracked open so he could keep tabs on any activity in the hallway.

Earlier he had alerted the military police to keep the area secure outside, and he was reasonably certain the night would be uneventful, at least from a safety angle. The only problem was he knew Lillie was right across the hall.

Dawson ordered a pizza in hopes of wooing her out of her room with food. Forty-five minutes later, he glanced out the window and saw the delivery car pull up in front of the building.

Footsteps sounded. Grabbing cash from his wallet, he stepped into the hallway only to find the general's aide standing in front of Lillie's door.

The captain's brow furrowed. "What are you doing here, Timmons?"

Lillie's door opened. She appeared surprised to see Mark, which gave Dawson a moment of relief, but when she glanced at Dawson, her surprise turned to confusion.

"Evening, Lillie," he said, hoping to deflect the question he saw in her eyes.

"I found the flash drive." Mark ignored Dawson and dropped the small memory stick into her outstretched hand.

"Thanks. Where was it?"

"Stuck in the corner of your inbox. I saw it when I was searching for the plans for the museum."

The delivery guy hustled toward Dawson with a pizza in hand, making an awkward moment even more complicated. Dawson paid the driver, who quickly scurried back to his car as if even he sensed the growing tension.

Unwilling to let the general's aide have the last word, Dawson forced a smile. "Hungry? I've got more pizza than I can eat."

Lillie glanced from Dawson to Mark and then back to Dawson again. He continued to hold the outstretched box of pizza, feeling like a third wheel. His hope was that the aide would get the hint and leave, although from the way Mark puffed out his chest and sidled closer to her room, Dawson could end up being the odd man out.

"I've already eaten." Lillie's emphatic statement shattered his hopes for the night. The aide seemed equally deflated.

"Now, gentlemen, if you'll both excuse me, I need to get back to work." Confidently in control, Lillie turned on her heel and retreated into her room. The door shut with a definite slam, followed by the clink of the dead bolt falling into place. Evidently she really did want to be alone.

Mark harrumphed and appeared somewhat exasperated with her abrupt departure. He stared at the door for a long moment before he looked over his shoulder at Dawson. "Enjoy your dinner."

Once the aide had left the building, Dawson placed a portion of the pizza on a paper plate and walked across the hall. He tapped on Lillie's door.

She opened it ever so slightly. "Yes?"

"Just in case you get hungry later." He shoved the plate into her hands. "I'm staying across the hall. My cell will be on all night. Call me if you want to talk."

The rather bewildered look on her face made him smile. He reached for a loose strand of her hair and tucked it neatly behind her ear. "I won't bother you. Cross my heart."

Just as she had done earlier, he turned about-face and walked back to his room. After closing the door, he peered through the peephole.

Lillie stood staring down at the pizza. Then, as if her stomach had gotten the best of her, she reached for a slice and took a big bite. Even with the distortion of the peephole, he could still recognize the look of pleasure on her face as she licked her lips. Score one for the CID, Dawson thought as she returned to her room.

Maybe tomorrow she'd be more willing to talk to him. At least that's what he hoped. Tonight he'd stand guard and ensure she was safe.

Dawson wanted her to need him, but not only for protection. He was beginning to realize he wanted Lillie to need him in an entirely different way as well.

Try as she might, Lillie couldn't find anything on the flash drive that she hadn't seen with Dawson just a few nights ago. Nor did she find anything that indicated Granger Ford was confused or had falsified information, especially since Mr. Simpson had confirmed the story about the college boy in the bar.

Poring over the information, Lillie stayed up too late and hit Snooze when the alarm went off in the morning. Rushing to get to work, she didn't have time to knock on Dawson's door and thank him for the pizza. Before she pulled into the post headquarters parking lot, she saw him in her rearview mirror.

She appreciated his watchfulness and hadn't felt personally threatened in the night. Although she had thought too much about the three women from Atlanta who had gone missing and Granger Ford's death and the two local women who may have been MLK victims as well.

Her mother had been a victim, and for so long Lillie had refused to open that door. Better to feel abandoned than to come face-to-face with a heinous act of violence against someone she loved.

Seeing the contents of the box yesterday made her realize how much she had loved her mother. Lillie was beginning to realize her mother had loved her in return. Hopefully time would heal some of the wounds she had lived with for so long.

Once at her desk, the time passed quickly as she worked on reports General Cameron needed updated. Mark was equally busy and somewhat aloof this morning, although she was grateful he didn't talk about last night.

As much as Lillie tried to keep her mind on office matters, she kept thinking of Dawson and the way her ear had tingled when he'd touched her hair. She also thought about his kiss outside her parents' house and how her heart had almost stopped, which had scared her so much she had run back inside.

For so long she had guarded her feelings and walled herself off from people who got too close. Dawson had somehow broken through the barriers she had placed around her heart. She was vulnerable and had reacted irrationally yesterday at her house, when the storm had thrown her over the edge.

In hindsight, she knew Dawson hadn't started the fire or spray-painted the terrible words on her garage. He would never do anything to harm her. She needed to apologize to him and ask his forgiveness.

Dawson was a wonderful man who worked overtime to keep her safe. He deserved something better than a woman who needed to make her own peace with the past.

Hopefully, when the investigation was over, he would still be around. She couldn't imagine how she would feel if Dawson wasn't in her life.

Dawson tried to tie up the loose strings on the investigation once he got to work the next day. So many things still needed his attention.

The high-school guidance counselor called him back with information about the local students who had attended Georgia Tech around the time of Lillie's mother's death.

"Four girls were accepted to Tech during the years you mentioned to my secretary. Three of them graduated. One girl dropped out to get married. Only two male students were accepted. One enlisted in the military after his freshman year. The other boy moved to Nevada following graduation."

"And those were the only students?"

"That's right. I'll email their names and current addresses, if we have them on file."

"I appreciate your help."

"No problem. This is my last year before retirement. Not many folks need information that goes back to my beginning days in education." She chuckled, then paused.

"I just pulled up another file. A third male student was accepted to Tech. He didn't know if he'd have enough funding. Student loans eventually came through for him, and he received a sizable scholarship from a donor in town. The student was Bobby Webber."

Dawson jotted down the name.

"Bobby was a smart young man. We were all glad he was able to attend Georgia Tech. The family was poor. Three boys with three different fathers. Bobby was the oldest and excelled academically. The youngest boy was a slow learner. You'd never think they were from the same family except for their hair, which they inherited from their mother."

Dawson sat up. "What about their hair?"

"All three boys were carrottops. Bright red. Stood out in a crowd, if you know what I mean."

"What was the youngest boy's name?"

"Billy," she said. "Billy Everett."

SIXTEEN

True to her word, the guidance counselor emailed the names of the former Georgia Tech students. Bobby Webber's current Colorado address was on the list.

Dawson punched in a long-distance number and waited until he heard Special Agent Kelly McQueen Thibodeaux's answer. "This is a voice from your past," he teased.

"How are you, Dawson?" Kelly was one of the best shots in the entire CID, maybe the army. She had married a captain from Fort Rickman, and they had both been transferred to Fort Carson, not far from where Bobby Webber now lived.

"I could use your help, Kelly."

"Shoot."

He told her about the investigation and gave her a brief rundown on what he needed. "Find out anything you can about Bobby Webber, especially whether he could have been the drunken college kid shooting off his mouth."

"I'll team up with a friend on the local police force and see what we can find."

As soon as he disconnected, Dawson got a message that Chief Wilson wanted to see him in his office.

"Yes, sir?"

"Pritchard just called. Florida State Highway Patrol apprehended Billy Everett in the Jacksonville area. He was hitching a ride on the interstate."

Finally the case seemed to be coming together. "Did they question him, sir?"

"They're holding him until someone from here can escort him back to Georgia. Pritchard is sending one of his men and asked if you could go along."

"The only problem is Ms. Beaumont's security. She's got a room at the Lodge so she doesn't have to return to her own residence in town."

"I'll authorize the military police to keep the facility under surveillance. You should be back on post tonight."

Much as Dawson didn't want to leave Lillie, he appreciated the chance to be the first to question Everett. He also wanted to ensure nothing happened during transport that would allow the suspect to escape. Especially after learning his brother had gone to Georgia Tech.

As Dawson left Fort Rickman to meet the local police officer escort, he considered calling Lillie and telling her he would be away from post for the remainder of the day. Chief Wilson had assured him the military police would keep the Lodge under surveillance, and Dawson was certain she would be safe while he was gone.

She hadn't wanted to see him last night. No reason for him to think she would have changed her mind. He decided to call her when he got back to post. Maybe she would join him for dinner at his BOQ.

Lillie had taken the pizza bait last night. Tonight he would tempt her with rib-eye steaks, baked potatoes and cheesecake from the commissary.

Although he would probably need more than a good meal to soften her heart. Lillie believed in the Lord. If only God would help her resolve her past. Maybe the Lord would help Dawson as well, yet he had been away from his faith for so long. Dawson wasn't sure the Lord—or Lillie—would want anything to do with him again.

Lillie and Mark worked without a break until noon, when he picked up burgers at the Post Exchange food concession. Tom Reynolds stopped by to go over plans for the military gym membership. Seeing how busy they were dealing with last-minute details for the museum building project kickoff, he offered to return later in the week.

General Cameron called Lillie into his office in the afternoon. "I got a phone call from Chief Wilson. Looks like they have a suspect in custody in Jacksonville."

"Florida?"

"Actually, he's from Freemont." The general glanced down at the note he had made. "The suspect's name is Billy Everett. Special Agent Timmons is bringing him back to Georgia."

Lillie was relieved Billy was in custody and proud of Dawson for his role in the investigation. "Thank you for letting me know, sir."

"It's been a long time coming, but you'll soon have closure on all of this."

By six o'clock, Lillie was worn out and ready to leave the office. Mark had left ahead of her with his workout bag in hand, headed for the gym. She decided to call Dawson, hoping he might be back in the area by now.

As much as Lillie wanted to go home, she had the room at the Lodge for one more night. Dawson would probably be tired from his long day, and he might want to get together for dinner. Nothing fancy, but Lillie wanted to hear what had happened and if he had learned anything new from Everett.

Her call to Dawson went to voice mail. She decided not to leave a message. There was so much for her to explain, plus she needed to apologize for acting like a spoiled child instead of a rational adult.

Once back at the Lodge, Lillie changed into jeans and a sweater, knowing she needed fresh air after being cooped up in the office all day. She knocked on Dawson's door, and when he didn't answer, she called his cell again. Either he was out of range or had turned off his phone.

Lillie knew a walk would do her good. She had a lot to think about concerning her mother's death and everything that would be brought into the open now that Everett was in custody. Plus, she was ready to see where her mother's remains had been uncovered.

"Oh, Lord, help me understand what happened. Maybe then I'll be able to put it all behind me and move on with my life."

She thought of Dawson, and of the future they might have together. Or was she being too optimistic?

A nature trail ran along the river. She headed north, enjoying the sunshine and the moderate temperature for January.

After seeing her mother's items in the box, Lillie wondered if Everett had broken in to steal her jewelry. Maybe her death had nothing to do with the murders in Atlanta or with the man who'd claimed to murder women and bury them in steel drums.

Lillie shivered as a cloud blocked the sun. The wind picked up over the water and whipped her hair around her face. She should have worn a heavier jacket. What had she been thinking? She was dressed for April instead of January.

In the distance, she heard the sound of earthmoving vehicles and realized she had walked almost to the site of the new museum. If she cut through the tall trees and bramble near the water's edge she would be able to see the construction area.

Wrapping her arms around her body, she tried to ward off the drop in temperature and the chilling reminder that her mother's body had been unearthed nearby.

Although she should turn around, Lillie kept moving forward, drawn to where the steel drum had been found. Just like everything else, she had closed off this part of her life and had never ventured to the water's edge.

For so long, she had wanted nothing to do with her mother. The thought of her own stubbornness wrapped around her and brought tears to her eyes. What kind of a daughter would exclude the memory of the woman who had given her life?

Tears fell as Lillie continued forward. The narrow pavement disappeared and led to a dirt path.

Time to go back to the Lodge.

She wiped her eyes and noticed a vehicle parked in the thickly wooded area.

A man stood nearby.

Her heart pounded a warning as her gaze cleared. The vehicle was a white Suburban, tinted windows, with an army decal on the bumper.

Fear clamped down on Lillie's chest. Her hand flew to her mouth. A twig snapped underfoot.

He startled at the sound.

From the look in his eyes, she knew he hadn't expected anyone to find him.

"What an odd coincidence, Lillie. I had planned to come after you tonight."

She ran. Behind her, the sound of his footfalls sent waves of terror to tangle along her spine.

She willed her legs to move faster. The overgrowth snagged her sweater. Branches grabbed her arms.

Where was the paved path she had walked on earlier?

Her foot caught on a root. She stumbled, righted herself and ran on.

His footsteps grew louder.

She pushed forward, hearing him pull air into his lungs. He was so close.

His hand grabbed her shoulder and sent her hurtling to the ground. She screamed, climbed to her knees and tried to scurry away.

"You can't run from me now, Lillie."

She screamed again as his hands wrapped around her neck, blocking the air from her lungs.

All she could think about was Dawson, who she had turned her back on yesterday. He had wanted to keep her safe, but she'd rejected him. Now Dawson would never be able to find her, and just like her mother, Lillie's body would someday be recovered by the water's edge.

SEVENTEEN

Traffic snarled along Interstate 10, delaying Dawson and the local Freemont cop. They arrived in Jacksonville at 5:00 p.m., during peak end-of-the-workday traffic and wall-to-wall grid-lock. By the time they walked into the police headquarters where Everett was being held, both men were out of sorts and knew they had to face more traffic on the return trip to Georgia.

Everett refused to answer any questions en route, and Dawson eventually let him sulk until they arrived back in Freemont.

Pritchard arrived at police headquarters, and both he and Dawson questioned the redhead repeatedly. The only infor-mation they learned was that Everett had done yard work for Lillie's mother.

"What about the photo of Irene Beaumont?" Dawson asked. "How did it get under the mattress in Granger's motel room?"

Everett crouched in his chair like a tortoise trying to hide within his shell. "Somebody put it there, but it wasn't me."

The redhead had also done yard work for the prosecutor and had overheard him talking on the phone about setting Granger up to take the rap. Again, Everett failed to provide the caller's name.

"The cops found a newspaper photo of you in Granger's room. Had he contacted you?"

"He tracked me down when he got out of prison. All I could tell him was the prosecutor set him up. Then Granger got shot, and I hitched a ride out of town."

"What about Roseanne and Valerie? Were you dating Roseanne? Did you kill her?"

Everett shook his head, his eyes wide. "No. You've got that all wrong. Roseanne hated small towns. She wanted to get a job in Atlanta. I told her how to thumb a ride and find a place to stay when she got to the city."

"Because you visited your brother when he was in college there?"

"Yeah, that's right."

Dawson leaned across the table and got in the punk's face. "Is your brother Bobby a killer?"

"Ah, man, you're crazy. Bobby wouldn't hurt anyone."

"How can you be so sure?"

"Because he tried to help me even when I didn't want his help."

Dawson looked at the skinny guy with greasy hair and a week's growth of beard, and knew he was telling the truth about his brother. Dawson wasn't sure he could trust Everett about anything else.

It was late by the time Dawson returned to the Lodge. He saw two military police officers on patrol when he pulled into the parking lot and felt assured they had kept the area under surveillance throughout the evening.

Climbing the stairs, he hoped Lillie would be awake and hear him. When her door remained closed, Dawson knew he needed to get some sleep. He would see her tomorrow, if not before the museum ceremony then immediately after the luncheon for the VIPs at the club.

Hopefully everything would smooth out between them,

but tonight, more than anything, Dawson wanted to wrap his arms around her and pull her close. She might not need him, but he needed her in his life. He had been alone for too long, and he was beginning to think he wanted her close for a long, long time to come.

Lillie groaned. Her head ached as if a giant sledgehammer had crashed into her skull. Her mouth tasted like bile, and she gagged. Trying to raise her hands, she realized they were bound. Her legs were as well.

Her eyes flew open. She was lying on a pile of rags in the corner of a garage. Tools hung from a pegboard overhead. Hunting trophies decorated the walls, along with a shellacked wooden paddle.

She squinted, hoping to decipher the letters—Greek letters—painted on the shiny wood. ΓΤ. Gamma Tau.

The words on the shirt Mr. Simpson had seen the boy in the bar wearing hadn't been Georgia Tech, but rather the name of a fraternity at nearby Georgia Southwestern, where she had gone to school.

Lillie peered at the only escape route—a small door on the far side of the garage that hung ajar, drawing in cold air. *Please, God.*

She couldn't think about the dropping temperature outside or how long she would have to hide in the bushes waiting for someone to find her. Staying here meant certain death, and more than anything, she wanted to live.

Dawson's face swam into view. She had so much to tell him about the good man he was and how he had been the only person to ever break down the wall she had built around her heart.

She hadn't wanted to let anyone in, until Dawson. Now she wanted him more than anything. If only he could find her. He probably thought she wasn't interested in seeing him again. She wanted to cry out at her own stupidity and self-centeredness.

Instead she tucked her chin to her chest and threw her left shoulder over her right, then flopped from her stomach to her back and continued to roll. Her shoulders and hips ached as they pounded against the cement floor, but she ignored the pain and forced herself to roll forward toward the partially opened door.

Footsteps.

Her heart exploded in her chest. She had to escape.

With a last push, she wiggled closer and cupped her chin around the bottom edge of the open door. Before she could inch it open, a force shoved the heavy oak, slamming the door into her neck.

She gasped. Pain radiated through her jaw.

He kicked her.

She screamed.

"What do you think you're doing?"

Instinctively, she curled into a fetal position, trying to protect herself. She saw the mud-covered boots as he struck her again and again. More frightening than his blows was the steel drum he rolled into the garage, identical to the one her mother had been buried in so many years ago.

Like mother, like daughter. Lillie would die tonight just as her mother had, buried alive where no one would ever find her.

EIGHTEEN

Before Dawson fell asleep that night, his cell rang. He checked caller ID and pushed the phone to his ear. "Hey, Kelly. Didn't take you long."

"I got one of my friends from the local police department to join me. We paid Mr. Webber a visit. The guy's squeaky clean. Runs a company that provides jobs for special-needs adults. He's also heavily involved in local charitable causes."

"Sounds like Burl Nelson from Freemont."

"Who?"

"Never mind."

"Mr. Webber says he's never touched alcohol, even in his youth. His pastor vouched for him. My gut feeling is he's telling the truth. I'd say you've got the wrong guy if you think he's involved in anything suspect."

"Thanks, I owe you. How's Phil?"

"Handsome as ever."

"You two ever plan to come back to Georgia?"

"Depends on Uncle Sam. Tell everyone in CID headquarters I said hello. Colorado is golden. Come visit sometime."

Dawson hung up feeling somewhat let down. Grateful though he was for Kelly's help, he had hoped Bobby Webber would turn out to be the missing link. The guidance counselor had mentioned another brother. He'd have Pritchard check it out.

At least Billy Everett was in custody, and something was bound to break soon. Everything pointed to wrapping up the case in the next day or so. Dawson should feel optimistic, but when the investigation concluded, he and Lillie would go their separate ways, which wasn't what he wanted.

He thought again of Kelly and Phil Thibodeaux and their happily-ever-after marriage. Was that what he wanted for his life? Or was he acting like a crazy fool for thinking an ex-con's son could find a woman who loved him despite his father and his past?

"Sweet Lillie, come to Mama. Your daddy's here."

She turned and saw her father, the man who traveled, or so Mama said. He laughed and so did Mama. Scooping Lillie into her arms, her mother kissed her cheek.

"A storm's coming, Irene. Put the child to bed." His voice.

"It's early, dear."

"But I don't have long tonight. Do as I say so we'll have enough time together."

"I want to stay with you, Mama."

"Hush, darling. We'll be together in the morning."

Only no one was there when the storm passed.

"Lillie?" Another voice broke into her memories. This one in present day and close to her ear. Stale breath, rough hands.

"You can't get away from me this time."

He shoved her into the drum. She fought and kicked and screamed, but he was too strong for her. His fist crashed into her chest. Everything swirled around her.

With a loud *clang,* the lid crashed down into place. Lillie cringed with each horrific jolt as he pounded it shut. Darkness surrounded her.

She gasped for air.
How long before she'd die?
Too long.
Oh, Dawson, where are you?

NINETEEN

Ever so quietly, Dawson eased the door to his room closed the next morning as he left the Lodge so as not to disturb Lillie, sleeping across the hall. She would have to be up soon enough to get ready for work.

Even though he wasn't fully convinced Billy Everett was the killer, Dawson still felt confident Lillie was safe on post. The military police were on alert and checking each vehicle that passed through the main gate.

Not that something couldn't happen on federal property, yet chances were good Granger's murderer was a civilian from off post who wouldn't venture onto the military garrison.

Chief Agent in Charge Wilson had assigned CID personnel and military police to cover the ceremony at the museum this morning. With the number of wealthy businessmen and politicians in attendance, as well as the Freemont mayor and local officials, General Cameron wanted to ensure the VIPs could enjoy the ceremony in total safety.

Arriving on-site early, Dawson met up with Jamison near the raised special seating area. Both of them eyed the sky and the dark clouds in the distance.

"Looks like the weather might be a problem." Dawson stated what they both knew to be true.

"The general debated moving the ceremony to the auditorium on post."

"Which would have been a good idea."

Jamison nodded. "In hindsight. Although Karl Nelson asked to keep it out here. He wanted his construction crew to be able to hear the general's praise for what they are about to accomplish."

"I'd hate to see the weather bring everything to a halt, especially after all the preparations that have gone into today." Dawson thought of the hours Lillie had spent on the project. "Still, it's the general's call. Any idea what time the old man is expected to arrive?"

"Before long." Jamison checked his watch. "The ceremony is scheduled to start at oh-nine-hundred hours. My guess, he'll be here in the next few minutes."

By the time Lillie arrived at the construction site, Dawson would need to focus on the special guests. He wouldn't be able to talk to her until after the official program had concluded, and then only in passing. Following the ceremony, he had to proceed to the club and provide security at the luncheon.

With a few minutes to kill before the VIP vans arrived, Dawson jabbed Jamison's arm. "You'll never guess who I talked to last night?"

"Kelly Thibodeaux."

Dawson tried to hide his surprise. "Did she call you?"

Jamison laughed. "Only to ask if something was going on between you and the general's secretary."

"What?"

Jamison shrugged. "You know women have a sixth sense about matchmaking. Kelly heard something in your voice when you mentioned Lillie's name."

"I was merely bringing Kelly up to date on the case."

Jamison raised his brow and stared at Dawson. "So was she right?"

"About what?"

"Oh, come on, Dawson, stop playing games. I'm talking about you and the general's secretary. My mother-in-law thinks Lillie's charming."

Jamison's wife was the daughter of one of the colonels on post. "How is Michele?"

"She's fine, but you're changing the subject." Jamison chuckled as he turned to study the construction area. "I heard you brought Billy Everett back from Florida. What's he have to say?"

"Only that he doesn't know who killed Lillie's mom or Granger Ford."

Jamison sniffed and then glanced back at Dawson. "I'm sorry about all this, Dawson. I told Wilson I was to blame for you taking the case in the first place."

Dawson held up his hand. "We've been over this before, Jamison. The problem's mine. I told him you were only doing your job."

"Maybe, but I still feel responsible." He patted Dawson's back and then walked off to check the VIP area.

Glancing at the dark clouds, Dawson thought about his father, who had been absent from his life. Growing up, he believed his mother had been the problem and not his dad.

Eventually, he'd realized his mother had done her best under difficult circumstances. Life wasn't fair, and some people managed better than others. Dawson had worked hard to ensure her woe-is-me way of looking at life didn't rub off on him.

No wonder he had created an imaginary father whom he tried to emulate. Lillie was right. Dawson had worked construction as a teen because of his dad.

Until the accident.

He should have known trying to follow in his father's footsteps could be his undoing.

The army had offered him another way out and a chance to make a success of his life, to do something right and make a difference. If only the JAG would find him innocent of any wrongdoing.

He glanced at his watch, wanting to call Lillie and hear her voice. No doubt she was still at post headquarters, working on last-minute details the general needed prior to the ceremony. Dawson couldn't interfere. Not now.

A handful of folks from town had already arrived and started to find their seats in the reviewing stands. The bus, transporting the Fort Rickman Army Band, pulled into the parking lot. The director studied the sky as if he too was worried about the storm.

What a shame to have everything come to a halt before the ceremony had even started. Although the weather should never be ignored. Dawson thought back to the day he'd been digging the ditch. No one had realized rain the night before had weakened the ground until the sides of the ditch collapsed in on Dawson.

He shook off the memory and turned his gaze to the pit in the middle of the construction site, where pylons and a crisscross of rebar established the layout of the building's basement foundation. A front-end loader and two dump trucks sat parked nearby.

Glancing over his shoulder, Dawson spied the caravan of vehicles, carrying the visiting dignitaries, pull into the makeshift parking area behind the bleachers. The VIPs disembarked, chatting among themselves as they made their way to the reviewing stand.

As people gathered in the stands, the band took up its position on the field and, after a brief warm-up, began to play military march music. The visitors kept time by tapping their feet or clapping their hands. The crowd seemed ready to enjoy the celebration. All was going well except for the approaching storm and General Cameron's absence.

Dawson checked his watch once again before glancing at the surrounding bleachers to ensure Lillie had not yet arrived.

In the distance, he spied the car carrying the commanding general. A flag with two red stars fluttered from the front bumper.

All eyes were on the sedan when it pulled to a stop at the side of the VIP area. The general's aide rode in the front passenger seat. Mark exited the vehicle and rounded to the far side to assist General Cameron with the door he had already opened.

Karl Nelson parked behind the general. He stepped from his car and shook hands with two men standing nearby. The general and Nelson exchanged greetings and chatted with a number of people as they walked through the growing crowd of onlookers. The general climbed the platform to where the distinguished guests were seated on folding chairs. Karl waved to the local townspeople in the bleachers before he joined Cameron.

Dawson expected to see Lillie's car. She would probably be wearing the attractive and very appropriate brooch that would draw the attention of many of the women in the crowd.

The post adjutant walked to the microphone and welcomed the dignitaries and local guests to the morning ceremony. He invited the visitors to stand as the band played the national anthem.

Dawson pulled his hand to his forehead in salute along with those in uniform. The women and civilians covered their hearts with their right hands. Many of the invited guests sang along with the words they knew so well.

At the conclusion of the anthem, Dawson scanned the crowd, but he still couldn't find Lillie. The chaplain stepped forward and prayed for God's protection for the construction crews working on the project and for good weather to see the museum completed in a timely manner.

Although heartfelt, his prayer seemed a bit late in coming as the sky continued to darken and the wind gathered strength. Many of the folks in the bleachers hustled to their cars in anticipation of the approaching storm.

The adjutant returned to the microphone and introduced the commanding general. Cameron leaned down to talk privately with Karl. The general pointed to the storm clouds. Karl waved his hand, his negative response easy enough to read.

A number of the dignitaries whispered among themselves, their faces drawn and eyes wide as they too studied the sky.

Dawson recognized a state representative from the local area. He helped his wife slip into her raincoat and then escorted her off the platform. General Cameron turned and watched them hurry toward the waiting vans.

A bolt of lightning cut across the horizon. A clap of thunder followed almost immediately.

Without glancing at his prepared speech, the general leaned into the microphone. "Ladies and gentlemen, the weather seems to be working against us today. For the safety of all, please return to the vans or your private vehicles. We will have to cancel the ceremony planned for this morning and move to the Fort Rickman Club. I'll join you there shortly."

Another bolt of lightning and the accompanying crack of thunder punctuated the general's remarks and hurried the people away from the metal stands. Before most folks reached their cars, the sky opened, and fat drops of rain pummeled the earth.

More concerned than ever, Dawson sought out the general's aide. "Where's Lillie?"

"She never showed up at work today. I thought she was with you."

Icicles of fear punctured Dawson's heart. "Didn't she call to say what had happened?"

Mark steeled his eyes. "I doubt she'd tell me much of anything after she spent the night with you."

Dawson wanted to grab the guy by the lapels and beat some manners into his affected grin.

"She didn't spend the night with me. Why would you think that? There's nothing going on between us. Besides, Lillie's not even sure she wants to talk to me at this point."

The aide raised his brow. "You're serious, aren't you? You really don't know where she is?"

"I wouldn't joke about Lillie's safety."

"I'm heading back to the club with General Cameron. I'll let you know if she arrives."

"Contact post headquarters. Maybe she's at the office by now."

"Will do. I'll get back to you as soon as I hear anything."

Dawson reached for his phone and speed-dialed Lillie's cell. His stomach tightened when an automated voice stated the number was not in service.

Standing in the midst of the mass of people running to their cars to get out of the rain, Dawson felt his heart drop lower than the cloud cover.

Where was Lillie? He had left post yesterday to apprehend Everett and hadn't seen her since.

Jamison helped the VIPs board the vans. Dawson hustled to his side. "Lillie never showed up for work today. I'm going to check the Lodge. If she's not there, I'll drive to her house in Freemont in case she went home. Cover for me at the club. I'll get there when I've located Lillie and know she's okay."

"Don't worry. We can handle it. I'll be praying you find her."

A lump formed in Dawson's throat. He wanted to thank Jamison, but he didn't know what to say in response to his offer to pray.

Looking back on the construction site, Dawson saw the giant earthmoving equipment standing idle at the edge of the deep pit. All around him, people were running for cover.

Without anyplace else to turn, he followed Jamison's lead. *"Lord, help me find Lillie."*

Then he climbed in his car and headed to the Lodge.

In Dawson's heart of hearts, he knew there was only one reason why Lillie wasn't at the ceremony today. Someone had her. Someone who wanted to do her harm.

Dawson stamped down on the accelerator, knowing he had to find Lillie before it was too late.

TWENTY

Lillie's eyes blinked open. Darkness surrounded her along with agonizing pain and bone-chilling cold. Her spine was twisted, her head crushed against metal, her legs bent up.

Earlier her hands had been tied behind her back. Now she moved her fingers, surprised they responded and equally surprised by the rush of fear that swept over her at the sound of distant thunder.

Nausea overcame her. She swallowed back the swell of bile, refusing to think of the storm or the smell of wet earth that filled her nostrils and clogged her throat.

A boom of thunder startled her. She jerked. Her cheek scraped the rough metal drum. The top of her head jammed against the lid.

Pushing her feet off the bottom of the container, she pressed her weight upward, hoping to force the lid open.

A thunderous crash shook the earth and sent waves of terror sweeping through her.

She thought once again of that night long ago when she had run on four-year-old feet along the hallway. "Mama," she had cried over and over again until the door opened. She had heard the man's voice just before the door closed again. No one had saved her that night, just as no one could save her now.

"No," she screamed as another wave of thunder bellowed overhead.

En route, Dawson called the Lodge and told the manager to meet him on the second floor with the master key.

Screeching to a stop in front of the entrance, he climbed the stairs two at a time, took the key from the manager's hand and ran along the hallway to Lillie's room.

He pounded on the door. "Lillie, open up."

Without waiting for an answer, Dawson shoved the key in the lock and raced into the room.

His heart stopped.

Her purse and cell phone were on the small writing desk. Her laptop was open. He clicked it back to life and checked the history. The last time she had been online was yesterday afternoon.

Leaving the small sitting area, he hurried into the adjoining bedroom, noting the neatly made bed and the outfit she had worn yesterday hanging in the closet. A blue suit, upon which she had already pinned the patriotic brooch, hung nearby.

No one could have gotten to her at the Lodge. Dawson had kept his own door open and watched the hallway from the couch where he had spent the night.

Lillie hadn't slept in the bed. Someone must have taken her earlier in the day, before Dawson returned from Florida.

Leaving the Lodge, he called Pritchard and filled him in. The cop promised to check her Freemont home and get back to Dawson.

The aide still hadn't called. Dawson drove to post headquarters, but when he entered the general's suite, it too was empty.

He called the military police and alerted them, but he didn't know where to tell them to look.

Her folks? He called the McKinneys' number and grimaced when Lillie's foster dad answered the phone.

"Sir, this is Special Agent Timmons."

"Oh, Dawson, I was planning to call you. I wanted to apologize for my actions Sunday afternoon. I was worried about my daughter and acted like a stupid fool, which is what Lillie called me."

The tension in Dawson's neck eased. "So Lillie's there with you?" He couldn't explain how she had gotten to their house since her car was parked at the Lodge, but Dawson wouldn't worry about that now. Just so she was safe.

"Lillie was right," Mr. McKinney continued. "I was a fool. You're a good man, Dawson, and Lillie cares for you a lot."

As much as he wanted to discuss the last statement with Mr. McKinney, Dawson had to ensure Lillie was all right. "Sir—"

"I hope you'll accept my apology. Lillie told me your father had been wrongly accused. A terrible travesty and then to have his death follow so soon after you two had just reconnected."

"Thank you, sir. I hate to cut you off, but could I speak to Lillie?"

"She's not here. I'm sure she's at work. You haven't seen her?"

"I'll keep looking, sir."

"She's all right, isn't she?"

"Right now I'm not sure of anything, sir. Just pray I can find her."

TWENTY-ONE

Dawson didn't know where to turn. Every place he looked for Lillie was a dead end. He wanted to scream to the heavens and beg the Lord to help him. But why would God listen to him now?

The few times Dawson had attended services when he was a new recruit, the chaplain had talked about a compassionate and merciful God.

If the Almighty truly was merciful, wouldn't He care about Lillie's well-being?

Think of her need, Lord, and not my own selfishness.

Dawson retraced the route he had taken earlier, not sure where he would end up. The first wave of the storm had passed with a downpour of rain and accompanying lightning.

Lillie feared storms. Wherever she was, she was frightened. Dawson was frightened too. Not for himself, but for the beautiful woman whose life had been somehow entwined with his since childhood.

Yet it had taken Granger's death to bring them together.

Oh, God, please, Dawson begged again. *Help me find her.*

Lillie had closed her mother out of her life and had only recently realized her mistake. If she wanted to be close to her mother again, where would she go?

A heaviness slipped over Dawson's shoulders.

The night they met, Lillie had said she hoped someday to be strong enough to visit the spot where the steel drum and Irene's decomposed body had been found. It wasn't far from the main road. Dawson put on his turn signal as he approached the turnoff. The narrow side road wove through a forest of hardwoods that hugged the river's bank.

Dawson took the turn too fast. The rear tires hydroplaned on the wet pavement. He eased up on the gas until the car straightened and then increased his speed. The wind whipped whitecaps on the churning water to his right, now muddied by the rain and runoff.

When the pavement finally ended, Dawson got out of his car and glanced out over the river, knowing Lillie wouldn't have done anything foolish.

He refused to allow such nonsense to fill his head. Instead, he turned to stare at the underbrush. The sounds of the forest surrounded him along with another sound that floated through the air.

The whine of a diesel engine. Not military, but some type of a construction vehicle. Surely Nelson hadn't allowed his men to work when another storm was moving into the area. As if to prove his point, a streak of lightning punctuated the sky.

Dawson cut through the bramble and emerged in the clearing. In the distance stood the now-empty bleachers and reviewing stand. The bunting that had covered the VIP area hung limp from the rain.

Scanning the cordoned-off worksite, Dawson saw a front-end loader move across a cleared stretch of land. The guy at the controls was a fool to be out in the elements with the threat of lightning overhead.

Even from where he stood, Dawson could see the tops of the steel pylons that, once buried, would provide a strong foundation for the new building. As he watched, the loader dumped a bucket of dirt into the gaping hole. The side of the pit crumbled under the vehicle's weight.

The memory of the collapsed earth sent fear roiling through Dawson's gut. The guy on the track didn't realize how easily the side of the pit could collapse, sending him and his vehicle crashing down the embankment.

"Stop," Dawson yelled. His words caught in the wind. He waved his arms and started to jog across the expansive clearing.

The temperature had dropped, and his leg ached. Each step sent pain down his calf. Despite his awkward gait, he pressed on.

Where was Karl Nelson? Probably eating lunch with the bigwigs, never realizing what was happening on the construction site. Not knowing Nelson's number, he phoned Mark's cell. The call went to voice mail.

"This is Dawson Timmons, CID. I know you're with the VIPs. Tell Karl Nelson to get over to the construction site before one of his men gets electrocuted in the storm."

Drizzling rain started to fall. Dawson squinted through the mist. The man at the switches was big and built. To add to his stupidity, he was working the machinery without a hard hat. The guy paused for a moment to wipe his hand across his bald head. He glanced up, for the first time, seeing Dawson.

"Get away from the worksite. Take shelter from the storm." Surely the guy would stop once Dawson had his attention, but instead of stopping, the man threw the vehicle into Reverse.

Dawson's phone vibrated in his hand. Raising it to his ear, he expected to hear the aide's voice. Instead Kelly McQueen Thibodeaux's words tumbled one after another.

"I failed to mention that Bobby Webber talked about his

middle brother, Tommy. He graduated from Georgia Southwestern."

"Kelly, it's a bad time."

"Wait, Dawson. Here's the thing. Tommy's fraternity—Gamma Tau—went to Atlanta each year to party over the MLK weekend."

The pieces Dawson had been struggling to connect suddenly came together. Tommy was the missing brother and the missing link in the two murders.

He pushed the cell closer to his ear. "Call CID headquarters at Fort Rickman. Tell them I'm at the museum construction site and need backup. Now."

Disconnecting, Dawson unholstered his weapon.

"Stop," he screamed over the whine of the engine and the *clink-clank* of the treads.

Working the two control levers, the guy scooped up another bucketful of earth and drove straight for the pit.

As the loader neared, Dawson recognized the musclebound man at the controls.

Tom Reynolds, the manager of the Freemont gym, was Billy Everett's brother.

Lightning flashed overhead, yet the bodybuilder continued to push forward, seemingly intent on filling in the foundation.

Dawson glanced down. His heart lurched. A buzzing sounded in his ears. His gut tightened as realization hit him full force.

A steel drum lay at the bottom of the pit, half-buried by dirt. One more dumped load, and the drum would be completely covered.

Dawson had to get there first.

He knew what he'd find when he opened the drum.

Dead or alive, Dawson knew he'd find Lillie.

* * *

Dawson fired two rounds.

One hit Tom's leg. He fired back, grazing Dawson's arm.

The Glock slipped through Dawson's fingers and dropped into the dirt far below.

Half sliding, half falling, he slipped and skidded and tumbled down the pit until he reached the steel drum.

His hands clawed at the dirt. He had to free Lillie.

Dawson tugged on the lid. It failed to open.

Frantically, he searched for something—anything—to use as a wedge. Spying a piece of rebar, he raced forward.

The wet Georgia clay clung to his shoes and sucked him down like quicksand. He tripped and then righted himself.

Grabbing the twisted metal, he retraced his steps.

The earth rumbled overhead.

The grinding sound of the diesel engine was deafening. Dawson couldn't hear, couldn't think, all he knew was that he needed to open the drum.

"Oh, Lillie."

Using the rebar, he pried at the lid. The lip gave way ever so slightly, and the edge started to pull free.

Metal scraped against metal.

He looked up just as the bucket tilted and a wall of dirt crashed down upon him. Dawson inhaled the cloying earth and thrashed at the free fall of debris.

Blinded by the dirt, he flailed his arms. His lungs burned like fire.

God, please.

The engine died. In its place, he heard laughter.

Wiping his sleeve over his eyes, Dawson glanced up. The muscular bodybuilder stood on the edge of the pit. Blood darkened his pant leg.

"You're a fool, Dawson. One more bucketful of soil, and they'll never find you or the steel drum."

"You…" Dawson gasped for air. "You killed three prostitutes in Atlanta."

The beef shook his head. "My brother killed them."

"Billy?"

"He's too dumb."

And Bobby was too smart.

"You got drunk and told your story to a bar owner in Atlanta." Dawson needed answers. "He said you were wearing a college T-shirt. Only it didn't say Georgia Tech. It said Gamma Tau, your fraternity."

Tom stopped laughing. "Maybe you're smarter than I thought."

"You mentioned your brother." Dawson realized his own mistake. "Not a biological sibling, but your fraternity brother."

A smirk spread across Tom's full face. "The cops, the town, no one suspected who the murderer was."

"What about Granger Ford?"

"I had to kill him. He was getting too close to the truth."

"And you ran Lillie off the road."

"Only to scare her, but she kept digging for information."

With a groan, Tom hoisted himself back into the cab of the front loader and settled onto the padded seat.

The engine roared to life.

Dawson groped for his weapon, his fingers burrowing through the mud. Relief rushed over him when his hand touched the cool metal.

He raised the Glock.

Tom came into view.

Dawson squeezed the trigger and fired.

TWENTY-TWO

Dawson swept away the dirt that covered the drum. He clutched the rebar and pried off the lid. His heart hitched when he looked inside.

Lillie lay folded upon herself like a rag doll.

"Oh, honey." Grabbing her shoulders, he gently lifted her free.

Please, Lord, let her be alive.

Feeling for the artery in her neck, he was rewarded with a faint pulse and gasped with relief.

She was still alive.

His euphoria was short-lived, washed away when the loader rumbled back to life.

Glancing up, he expected to see Tom.

Instead, he saw the bucket suspended overhead. With a screech of metal, the load dropped. Dawson hunched over Lillie to protect her from the deluge of rock and soil and bramble.

The machine reversed and disappeared from sight. Dawson had to get Lillie out of the pit. Wrapping his arm around her waist, he dragged her up the fresh mound of dirt.

His feet slipped. He struggled to move forward.

Holding her close with one hand, he used the other to grab at the roots and debris tangled in the earth. They had to be clear of the pit before the next load of soil rained down upon them.

Dawson willed himself to keep moving, finding footholds that propelled him forward. His fingers locked on anything that would support his weight and Lillie's.

The sound of the diesel engine grew louder.

Finding a small ledge of packed earth, he tucked her behind him. The undercarriage of the loader appeared overhead. Dawson strained to see who was at the controls while his fingers curled around his weapon.

Karl Nelson leaned over the edge. Eyes bulging, hair disheveled and matted with mud.

"She has to die," he screamed over the drone of the engine.

Anger welled up within Dawson. "You killed her mother."

"I didn't have a choice."

Karl's face reddened with rage. "My father wanted to divorce my mother and marry his lover. I couldn't let that happen. He built Nelson Construction Company for me." He jammed a finger against his chest. "Why would I share my inheritance with his bastard child? My father did everything for everyone else, but he ignored me when I told him to get rid of Irene."

"They met in Atlanta, didn't they, Karl?" Dawson moved protectively in front of Lillie. "You saw them together over the MLK weekend."

"Their love child was born nine months later. For three years, I went to Atlanta to drown my sorrows. Each time my anger made me kill."

"Then you came after Irene. There was a storm that night."

Karl sneered. "I went to her house. She thought my father was at the door. When I told him later, his weak heart couldn't take the shock."

The construction boss disappeared from sight.

The idling engine throttled up, the sound deafening. The loader moved closer to the edge. The bucket rose overhead.

The cab came into view. Dawson raised his weapon and fired.

Karl grabbed the arm in the front loader.

The loader shifted. One track sank into the wet and weakened soil. The side buckled with the weight.

The edge gave way, and the huge machine rolled, releasing Karl's body. He fell headfirst against the steel pylon. The front loader teetered for a long moment and then, with a loud groan, crashed down on top of him.

Clawing his way up the last few feet, Dawson lifted Lillie free of the pit. He laid her on the ground, hearing the sirens in the distance.

Help was on the way.

Too late for Karl. But would they be in time to save Lillie?

TWENTY-THREE

Dawson stood outside the ICU, looking into Lillie's room. Pale as death, she lay unmoving on the bed. Wires hooked her to machines that monitored her heart rate and oxygen level. Dawson's only medical training was battlefield emergency triage, but even he knew the odds weren't good that Lillie would survive.

At the construction site, the EMTs had worked feverishly to stabilize her so she could survive the short ride to the hospital.

Because of his grazed arm and the amount of dirt he had inhaled, they transported Dawson in the same ambulance with Lillie. Being that close as they worked to keep her alive had almost been his undoing.

The sirens had screamed, clearing traffic and causing Dawson's heart to lodge in his throat, where it had remained ever since.

The phone call to her parents had been worse than walking into a minefield in Iraq. To their credit, the McKinneys hadn't blamed him. In fact they'd thanked him for saving her life.

Only her life still hung in the balance.

General Cameron and his aide had arrived almost as soon as the ambulance had pulled up at the hospital. Both men were shaken when they saw Lillie's seemingly lifeless body wheeled into the E.R.

The general had talked to a number of the medical personnel, trying to find out more information, but no one knew what would happen in the next few hours.

To their credit and even without the commanding general's promptings, the medical personnel worked quickly to transport her to the ICU where Dawson now stood.

He heard footsteps in the hallway and turned to see Jamison. His buddy's face reflected the fear that ate at Dawson's gut. If anything happened to Lillie, he wouldn't survive. At least not emotionally. He might go through the motions, but under the surface, he'd be a broken man, unable to move forward.

"I came as soon as I could." Jamison grabbed his shoulders in an embrace that revealed the depth of their friendship and his own concern for Lillie. "What's the prognosis?"

Dawson choked on the words. "Her…her chances aren't good. Being out all night in the cold. Lack of oxygen. Her lungs are filled with fluid. She's spiking a fever that they can't bring down. Right now, the pneumonia is her biggest problem. She's on a ventilator that's pushing oxygen into her lungs, but they're also worried about her kidney function."

An ICU nurse scooted past them and entered Lillie's room. She hung a new bag of antibiotics and adjusted the mechanical pump to ensure the proper flow of medication into Lillie's bloodstream.

Leaving the room, she smiled weakly at Dawson. "Agent Timmons, there's nothing you can do right now. We won't know anything until the antibiotics start to work. I'll call you if her condition changes."

"I don't want to leave her side."

Jamison squeezed his shoulder. "I brought the change of clothes you keep in the office and your Dopp kit. Why don't you find a shower and clean up, otherwise the janitorial service will have to work overtime."

Dawson looked down at the red clay that caked his shoes. His white shirt was stained with blood, and he didn't need a mirror to know dirt matted his hair and probably covered his face as well.

"There's a shower you can use at the end of the hall," the nurse offered, her eyes encouraging. "Packages of fresh toiletries and towels are on the shelf."

"When Lillie comes to, she won't want to see all that dirt," Jamison added, which convinced Dawson to follow his friend's advice. He didn't want anything to remind Lillie of what she had just endured.

The hot shower eased his sore muscles, but it did little for his outlook. He scrubbed the light flesh wound on his arm that he'd refused to let the medics treat. Later there would be time for him. Right now he was worried about Lillie. He'd never felt so helpless, and he knew her recovery rested solely in the hands of the medical team.

The nurse caught up to him in the hallway and covered his skinned flesh with antibiotic ointment and a thick four-by-four bandage. "Have one of the docs look at it tomorrow."

He found Jamison in the ICU waiting room. "The McKinneys arrived a few minutes ago. They saw Lillie and are in the chapel now."

"I...I should talk to them. The nurse said she'd call my cell if there's any change in Lillie's condition."

"How 'bout we get your shoulder treated first."

"It's already been taken care of."

The two special agents walked silently along the hospital corridors until they came to double doors and a sign that read *Peace be to you.* Jamison stood back so Dawson could enter.

A large bronze mosaic hung on the wall behind the wooden altar. A giant sun with streaming rays of light was depicted in tiny tiles pieced together into a tranquil scene of a country field and meandering brook. Dawson thought of Mr. McKinney's farm and the quiet farmland where Lillie had grown up.

"Oh, Dawson."

He turned to see Mrs. McKinney. Her face was wrapped in worry, but she opened her arms and pulled him close. Touched by the affection he sensed in her embrace, his eyes stung, and he bit down on his cheek to keep his emotions in check.

"We heard what you did to save our Lillie." She pulled back to look into his eyes. "How can we ever thank you?"

Unable to speak, he shook his head. Why would they thank him when Lillie was still in danger of losing her life?

Mr. McKinney stepped forward.

Dawson deserved everything the distraught father was about to say. Only Dawson wanted to apologize first. "Sir, I—"

The older man reached for Dawson's hand and then pulled him close. "Sarah and I have been thanking God that you found our daughter. Jamison told us what happened. In twenty-five years, no one has been able to learn the truth about Irene Beaumont's death until you got involved. I'm proud of you, son."

Once again, Dawson couldn't speak. He didn't deserve anyone's thanks or praise. He hadn't done anything that the other agents wouldn't have done.

"We've been praying for Lillie." Mrs. McKinney touched his hand. "Come sit with us, Dawson. There's power in prayer, and we want the Lord to know how much Lillie means to us." She squeezed his hand. "To all of us."

"Yes, ma'am."

Ushered forward, Dawson sat between Mrs. McKinney

and Jamison. Lillie's father was on the opposite side of his wife.

Totally out of his comfort zone, Dawson didn't know what to expect or what to do. Hopefully, he wouldn't have to express his thoughts out loud.

Within a few minutes, he realized each of the people gathered in the chapel was offering up private prayers to the Lord.

Mrs. McKinney closed her eyes and nodded a few times as if she could hear God's voice. Her husband wrapped his arms around his broad chest and stared at the floor, lost in his own world. Jamison reached for a Bible from a nearby table and turned to scripture for comfort.

Dawson stared at the mosaic and realized he had asked the Lord to help him find Lillie, but he hadn't thanked Him for doing just that.

Dropping his head into his hands, he struggled to clear his thoughts. *You...You had my back today, Lord, and Lillie's. Thank You doesn't seem to be enough to say, especially since I have more to ask of You. Heal her, Lord. Lillie doesn't deserve to die.*

Once again his eyes stung, but this time he knew he wasn't alone. In addition to the prayerful people sitting next to him, Dawson could feel the rays of God's love, just like the rays of the sun from the mosaic, flowing down around him.

Sensing the Lord's presence buoyed his spirits and gave him hope that Lillie would survive, but as the hours passed and her condition continued to fail, Dawson wondered if the feeling of peace that had flowed over him in the chapel had been his imagination instead of anything real.

The McKinneys believed in the power of prayer, but Dawson had turned his back on the Almighty for too long. Now when he most needed God in his life, Dawson couldn't trust anything, not even the Lord.

* * *

Eventually, the small group returned to the ICU waiting room. Jamison brought up sandwiches from the hospital cafeteria, although Dawson hadn't been able to eat.

Chief Wilson stopped by to check on Lillie's condition. He and Dawson stepped into the hallway to talk privately.

"The Freemont police got a search warrant for Karl Nelson's home. They found pictures of the three women from Atlanta along with a few shots of Irene Beaumont. The women were jammed into the drums, just like the photo found under Granger's mattress."

Dawson shook his head at the construction tycoon's depravity. "Evidently Mr. Nelson wanted to document his kills."

Wilson nodded. "I wonder if he showed his father the photos to prove what he had done. Medical records indicate Burl Nelson died of a heart attack not long after Irene's body was found."

"Karl didn't want to share his inheritance with his father's illegitimate child."

"Ironic that what he killed to prevent will eventually come true," Wilson said. "Karl never married and didn't have any heirs, so the Nelson Construction Company and all of its assets will go to Lillie. Plus, he owned the workout facility in Freemont Tom Reynolds ran. Not that money is important at a time like this."

"No, sir. The only thing that's important is Lillie's return to health."

"We're digging up the construction area, hoping to find the bodies of those three women from Atlanta. Once we do their families will have closure. That's because of your hard work." Wilson patted Dawson's back. "You did an outstanding job."

"Thank you, sir."

"There's one more thing."

"Yes, sir."

"I pulled your file and ran a check on your birth certificate, which verified the absence of your father's name on the official document."

"Yes, sir. That's what I told you and General Cameron."

Wilson nodded. "The JAG office confirmed you were within your legal authority to withhold his name on your recruitment papers since paternity had not been established at the time you entered the military. I'm sorry I had to follow up on that, Dawson, but I wanted to ensure this would never be a problem for you again."

"Does that mean Granger Ford's name will not be added to my record?"

"That's correct. Unless you request an official change to your file."

"I'll give that some thought."

"I told General Cameron the issue had been resolved. I also told him you are an excellent special agent and an asset to the division."

"Thank you, sir."

After the chief left, the nurse approached Dawson in the hallway. "We're going to see if Lillie can breathe on her own, if you want to tell her parents."

Dawson passed on the information. Mr. and Mrs. McKinney joined hands and prayed while Dawson stood nearby. The nurse's expression was downcast when she came back thirty minutes later. "She still needs the ventilator. The doctor wants to wait until later this evening before he tries again."

Dawson had never realized how hard waiting in the hospital could be. Every hour the McKinneys were allowed to see their daughter for a few minutes, but Lillie remained unresponsive. Mrs. McKinney always returned with tears in her eyes and cried softly in the corner while Mr. McKinney circled her with his arms and tried to comfort her with words of encouragement.

After their five o'clock visit, they went to the cafeteria, but only after Dawson promised to contact them if there was any change.

He paced the room, feeling the walls closing in around him. Since the construction accident, he had never liked confining spaces, but today his struggle was Lillie's fight to survive. He stopped in front of the large bank of windows and gazed at the gathering twilight outside. A gray pall that rivaled the weight of his own despair hung over the horizon.

Ready to turn away, he stopped as a patch of blue sky broke through the cloud cover, and rays of sunlight showered down upon the earth. Was God giving him a sign?

Granger had made his peace with the Lord and Dawson wanted to do the same, but there was one person with whom he needed to reconcile.

He raised his cell phone and plugged in a number. His mother's voice sounded tired when she answered.

After exchanging awkward pleasantries, Dawson got to the reason for his call. "When I was a little guy, you taught me to pray. Somewhere along the way we both stopped doing just that. I need your prayers today, Mom, for someone special. Her name is Lillie Beaumont."

As the hours ticked by, Dawson tried to convince the McKinneys to go home for the night, but they wanted to be close to Lillie. He couldn't blame them, since he felt the same way.

Eventually, they fell asleep on two reclining chairs in the

waiting room. Unable to relax, Dawson wandered the hallways and ended up at Lillie's room.

His heart lurched and fear chilled his soul when he saw the medical staff gathered at her bedside.

"She's breathing on her own," one of the nurses said as she left the room. "You can talk to her if you'd like. I doubt she'll respond, but she may be able to hear you."

Once the room cleared, Dawson approached Lillie's bedside. Using care not to disturb the tubes and wires, he took her hand in his.

"Lillie, it's Dawson. The nurse said I could talk to you, only I don't know where to start." He paused to decide what to tell her first.

"I can't hide how I feel about you any longer. You're the most wonderful woman in the world, and I...well, I love you and I want to be with you for the rest of my life." He smiled. "Actually even longer than that."

He rubbed her hand. "So you need to pull through and open your beautiful eyes."

She moaned.

Encouraged, he leaned closer. "Open your eyes, honey. Please, for me."

Her lashes quivered.

Oh, God, let her wake up.

A muscle in her neck twitched.

"Lillie, come on. You can do it."

She blinked. Slowly, her eyes opened. They were just as he remembered and as emerald-green as the fields around her father's house.

"Daw...son." She whispered his name.

"It's me, honey. I'm right here."

"You...you...saved...me."

"I'll never let anything get between us again. At least for as long as you want me around."

She nodded.

"Does that mean you *do* want me around?" he teased.

Her lips trembled and a tear ran down her cheek, causing his gut to tighten. The last thing he wanted was to make her cry.

"Look, honey. I'm probably saying too much—"

Weak as she was, her fingers squeezed his hand. "For… ever."

He bent down closer. "Did you say forever?"

She nodded ever so slightly. "Love you…forever."

Dawson's heart nearly exploded. Not from fear or worry, but from the realization that God had listened to his prayer. Lillie would pull through, he felt sure, and despite everything that had happened, they would have a future together.

Although he'd never known his father, Granger had in a very strange way brought them together. Despite their pasts, Lillie and Dawson could move beyond the pain and rejection of their childhoods because they had each other. More importantly, they had a God who was on their side and a love that would only grow stronger with time.

He touched her cheek, feeling the softness of her skin. Seeing a faint tinge of pink gave him hope that her pallor would soon improve.

"My timing's never been good." He smiled, feeling suddenly unsure of himself.

Then he looked into her eyes and any hesitation left him. "I said it when you were asleep, but just in case you didn't hear me, I need to say it again."

Her face filled with expectation.

"I love you, Lillie, and I want to spend the rest of my life trying to make you happy."

Then, in spite of the wires and machines, he lowered his lips and gently kissed her sweet mouth.

She sighed when he pulled back.

"I…love…you," she whispered before her eyes closed and she fell back to sleep.

EPILOGUE

The May sun warmed Dawson's back as he dug in the soil and planted another rosebush.

"You look like a farmer," Lillie teased. Kneeling nearby, she spread mulch around a group of flowering hydrangeas, their blooms as blue as the sky overhead.

Task completed, she sat back and studied the three-story museum that would be open within the week. "The weather should be perfect for the dedication."

Dawson left his shovel in the dirt and scooted next to Lillie, wondering if he'd ever tire of seeing the sunlight in her hair.

"Chief Wilson gave me the day off for the ceremony. He said I need to be sitting next to the woman who made this all possible."

Lillie smiled. "The plans had already been finalized. All I needed to do was ensure Nelson Construction completed the project on time."

"And under budget. You're a savvy businessman just like your father was."

She raised her brow playfully. "That would be *businesswoman,* Agent Timmons."

He laughed. "Yes, ma'am."

Wistfulness washed over her pretty face as she looked toward the nearby river. A path of dogwoods edged the stone walk that led to a picnic area near the water's edge.

"I dreamed about him last night," she said. "He and my mother were laughing. Then he reached for me and raised me into the air while I giggled and begged to go higher."

"I'm glad the good memories are returning. Have you told your mom?"

Lillie nodded. "She said her prayer has always been for me to know how much my biological mother and father loved me."

"The McKinneys are good people."

"And the best parents I could ever have."

"Did you contact the families of the three missing Atlanta women?"

"They all seemed touched by the college scholarships and the trees in each girl's memory. I told them they were planted near Irene's Garden."

Dawson looked at the etched plaque to Lillie's mother erected in the middle of the flowering bushes and rows of blooming plants. "It's a perfect memorial to her memory."

Lillie nudged his arm. "Plus it lets you play in the dirt. Dad said you're a farmer at heart. He also told me you were looking at land not far from their place."

"I wanted to surprise you. A hundred acres are for sale."

She studied him with pensive eyes. "You've decided to get out of the military?"

He shrugged. "I keep feeling a need to work the soil."

"Maybe you could go into landscaping," she teased, making him laugh.

"You have your construction company," he reminded her. "And your gym."

She held up her hand. "I'm putting both of them up for sale."

"Are you sure?"

"It's not what I want, Dawson."

He leaned in, his gaze intent on the fullness of her lips and the curve of her smile. "What do you want, Lillie?"

"I thought we discussed that when I was in the hospital."

"You needed time to heal, emotionally and physically."

She scooted closer. "I'm all better now."

"But this isn't the best time. I was thinking of a candlelight dinner and a roaring fire."

"It's too warm to build a fire." She looked around. "Besides, a farmer's wife likes fresh air and sunshine."

He tickled her chin. "You know what you want, don't you, Ms. Beaumont?"

"You do too, soon-to-be Farmer Timmons."

"What I want—" he reached for her "—is for you to be my wife."

Without saying yes, she wrapped her arms around his neck and molded into his embrace. All around them, flowers danced in the breeze from the river.

"We'll get married at the main post chapel," Lillie said. "And hold the reception in the ballroom at the museum."

He kissed her cheek and then her neck as she discussed plans for their wedding, while he enjoyed the softness of her skin and the fragrant scent of her perfume.

Dawson wouldn't mention that he had seen the wedding magazines at her parents' farmhouse or that Mr. McKinney had already clued him in on how women always got what they wanted.

After all, marrying Lillie was what Dawson wanted more than anything. He had given her time to heal and experience life without always looking over her shoulder.

Dawson had needed time to heal his relationship with his mother and grow in his faith. Both he and Lillie were stronger now and ready to start their new life together.

Tonight, after they had a candlelight dinner, he would slip

a ring on her finger and formally ask her to be his wife. But he already knew the answer. Their lives had been entwined, seemingly forever.

The storms of the past were over, and the future would be filled with sunshine and babies. Strong boys to help him on the farm and emerald-eyed girls who would steal his heart, just as Lillie had done the first time he saw her.

She continued to chatter, but then she stopped and smiled at him, her eyes making him think of lush green farmland and the home they would build on their new acreage.

Then thoughts of everything else left him and all he could think about was Lillie. Her lips on his, her arms holding him tight, the way their hearts beat in sync. They kissed and kissed and kissed again, while the sun warmed them and the gentle breezes wrapped them in a loving embrace.

* * * * *

Dear Reader,

I hope you enjoyed *THE GENERAL'S SECRETARY,* the fourth book in my Military Investigations series, which features heroes and heroines in the army's Criminal Investigation Division. Each story stands alone so you can read them in any order, either in print or as an ebook: *THE OFFICER'S SECRET,* book 1; *THE CAPTAIN'S MISSION,* book 2; and *THE COLONEL'S DAUGHTER,* book 3.

Abandoned by her mother when she was a child, Lillie Beaumont now works for the Fort Rickman commanding general. More than anything else, Lillie doesn't want to upset the perfect, albeit reclusive, life she has created for herself. But when a man is murdered on her front porch, she can no longer block out what happened long ago.

Special Agent Dawson Timmons is called in to investigate a murder that hits too close to home. Forced to expose a secret from his past, he must work with Lillie to solve not only one murder but a series of crimes that could jeopardize his military career. Before the truth can be revealed and healed, Lillie and Dawson must turn to the Lord in their need.

I pray for my readers each and every day. If concerns weigh you down, call upon the Lord. He is a God of mercy and forgiveness, and His love is unconditional.

I want to hear from you. Email me at debby@debbygiusti.com or write me c/o Love Inspired, 233 Broadway, Suite 1001, New York, NY 10279. Visit my website at www.DebbyGiusti.com.

And blog with me at:

www.seekerville.blogspot.com
www.craftieladiesofromance.blogspot.com
www.crossmyheartprayerteam.blogspot.com

As always, I thank God for bringing us together through this story.

Wishing you abundant blessings,

Debby Giusti

Questions for Discussion

1. What does the memory box symbolize in this story? Why did Lillie hide the box in the back of her closet, and what did she learn when she finally looked inside?

2. Karl Nelson said, "Sometimes the person we know best can cause us the most pain." How did that prove true in this story?

3. What was the significance of the child's drawing? Was that a turning point for Lillie?

4. When he was a young boy, Dawson had a bigger-than-life image of his father. When and how was that image shattered? By the end of the story, what had Dawson learned about his dad?

5. Why did Lillie feel the need to protect her heart? Is there something from your past that keeps you from living fully in the present?

6. Mr. McKinney was a man of faith, yet his comments about prison hurt Dawson. What did Lillie's father do when he realized his mistake? In your opinion, is it harder to forgive or to ask forgiveness?

7. How is the climax foreshadowed in this story?

8. Do you think Dawson eventually changed his military paperwork and claimed Granger as his father? Was Granger a heroic figure? If so, why?

9. How did the construction accident in Dawson's youth affect him? What did he learn from that incident that played a role in this story?

10. Granger Ford found Christ when he was in prison. Is Christian prison ministry important and does it lower the rate of recidivism, which is a problem in the U.S.? Has God ever called you to work in prison ministry? If so, share your experiences.

11. Before his death, Granger asked Lillie to free them from the past. In what way did she fulfill his request?

12. How does the setting enhance the suspense in this story? Does Lillie's fear of storms make her a more compelling character?

13. What did the mosaic in the hospital chapel symbolize to Dawson? Are there visual signs in your life that remind you of God's love?

14. What themes are explored in *The General's Secretary?* What have you learned from this story?

15. What was the significance of Irene's Garden? How did Lillie reach out to the families of the three murdered Atlanta women?

REQUEST YOUR FREE BOOKS!

2 FREE RIVETING INSPIRATIONAL NOVELS PLUS 2 FREE MYSTERY GIFTS

Love Inspired®
SUSPENSE

YES! Please send me 2 FREE Love Inspired® Suspense novels and my 2 FREE mystery gifts (gifts are worth about $10). After receiving them, if I don't wish to receive any more books, I can return the shipping statement marked "cancel." If I don't cancel, I will receive 4 brand new novels every month and be billed just $4.49 per book in the U.S. or $4.99 per book in Canada. That's a savings of at least 22% off the cover price. It's quite a bargain! Shipping and handling is just 50¢ per book in the U.S. and 75¢ per book in Canada.* I understand that accepting the 2 free books and gifts places me under no obligation to buy anything. I can always return a shipment and cancel at any time. Even if I never buy another book, the two free books and gifts are mine to keep forever.

123/323 IDN FVWV

Name	(PLEASE PRINT)	

Address		Apt. #

City	State/Prov.	Zip/Postal Code

Signature (if under 18, a parent or guardian must sign)

Mail to the Harlequin® Reader Service:
IN U.S.A.: P.O. Box 1867, Buffalo, NY 14240-1867
IN CANADA: P.O. Box 609, Fort Erie, Ontario L2A 5X3

Are you a subscriber to Love Inspired Suspense
and want to receive the larger-print edition?
Call 1 800-873-8635 or visit www.ReaderService.com.

* Terms and prices subject to change without notice. Prices do not include applicable taxes. Sales tax applicable in N.Y. Canadian residents will be charged applicable taxes. Offer not valid in Quebec. This offer is limited to one order per household. Not valid for current subscribers to Love Inspired Suspense books. All orders subject to credit approval. Credit or debit balances in a customer's account(s) may be offset by any other outstanding balance owed by or to the customer. Please allow 4 to 6 weeks for delivery. Offer available while quantities last.

LIS13

SPECIAL EXCERPT FROM
LOVE INSPIRED® SUSPENSE

Who was the mysterious woman in the woods?

Read on for a preview of the next book in the exciting
TEXAS K-9 UNIT *series,* DETECTION MISSION
by Margaret Daley.

Who am I?

She bent over the sink in the bathroom in her hospital room and splashed some cold water on her face. She studied herself in the mirror and didn't know the person looking back at her.

A sound coming from the other room invaded the quiet. She moved toward the door. But when two deep male voices drifted to her, she pressed her ear against the wood to listen.

"Where is she?"

"Who?"

"The patient who belongs in this room."

"I don't know. I'm here to clean her room. She wasn't in here when I arrived."

The sound of the two men talking about her sent her heartbeat racing. Why? It seemed innocent enough. But she couldn't calm the pounding beat against her chest. Her breathing shortened. She eased the door open an inch and had a pencil-narrow view into the room.

"I can come back another time. You'll have to ask the nurse where the patient is." The guy who was there to clean her room held a plastic bag in one hand.

The other man, just out of sight to the left, said, "I will."

Fear from somewhere deep inside her swelled to the surface. She tried to search her mind for any clue, however small.

But she couldn't move.

Why was she in the hospital?

Why were the police interested in her?

A suffocating pressure in her chest made it difficult to breathe. According to the nurse, the police had found her in the Lost Woods and she'd been in the hospital several weeks. When she was brought in, she'd slipped into a coma from a head injury. Why hadn't anyone reported her missing? Come forward to identify her?

A knock at the bathroom door caught her by surprise. She gasped.

"Are you all right in there?"

"Who are you?" she finally managed to ask.

"I'm Officer Lee Calloway with the K-9 Unit of the Sagebrush Police Department."

She opened the door a few inches. "Sagebrush? Where is that?" The large man, muscular in a dark navy blue police uniform, stepped back.

"In Texas, southwest of San Antonio."

"Who am I?"

The corner of his mouth hiked into a lopsided grin. "That, ma'am, is one of the questions I'm here to ask you."

Pick up DETECTION MISSION by Margaret Daley, available February 2013 wherever Love Inspired Suspense books are sold

Love Inspired SUSPENSE

RIVETING INSPIRATIONAL ROMANCE

FRAMED FOR TREASON

Former military woman Madison McKay had already been betrayed in work *and* in love. And when she's framed for a security breach at a top secret military facility, she's forced to trust special investigator Grant Deaver. But after she discovers that he's been deceiving her, everything will be torn apart unless Grant can convince her to trust him with her life...*and* her heart.

LOST INC.

By finding and helping the lost, these broken ex-military investigators heal

TORN LOYALTIES
by
VICKI HINZE

Available in February wherever books are sold.

www.LoveInspiredBooks.com

LIS44525